THE DUKE AND THE DJ

THE REBEL ROYALS BOOK 3

SHANAE JOHNSON

THOSE JOHNSON GIRLS

Diego Zhi Wen de Bernadino, the Duke of Mondego, stood before his assembled staff. It was a big day for the ducal estate. His father's ancestors had ruled over the estate for hundreds of years since sailing from Spain and staking a claim in the island nation of Cordoba.

The Mondegos were conquerors, leaders, fierce warriors who nobles and commoners alike turned to for guidance and protection. For generations, they'd held great amounts of land and governed over countless tenants. True, they'd plundered a few foes and even some allies, but they'd also invested in the land and its people and grown an empire.

Zhi was determined that now that the dukedom had passed down to him at the tender age of twenty-five, that tradition would continue. The guiding, protecting, and investing bit. Not the other more distasteful and dastardly side of his kinfolk.

"We have been charged with an awesome responsibility," he announced from his place on the grand staircase. "I know these are trying times, but we are the House of Mondego."

Pride and loyalty shone on the faces of his staff. The males tilted their chins up in deference. The women's smiles widened with honor. Zhi felt like a head coach in a locker room at halftime. He was certain that after his speech, his team would go out and conquer anything in their path.

"We have traditions to uphold," he continued. "So, we must buckle down and get to work. Best foot ever forward. Backward never."

It was the Mondego way. It was also the family motto. It had been brought over from their Spanish ancestors, though the Spanish words were more poetic. But, still, it did the trick. His staff was ready to move mountains under his guidance.

As Zhi went to put his best foot forward, a water drop fell on his nose. He looked up at the brown spot in the ceiling. He'd noticed it had spread since yesterday. In fact, it was spreading before his eyes.

In his periphery, he saw the chins of his staff tilt up, way up until they all were looking at the ceiling. And then a deluge poured down on his head. The light fixture next to the spot short-circuited, and they were all in darkness.

"I'll get the breaker."

"I'll get another bucket."

"I'll get a mop."

Covered in water from his head to his toes, Zhi couldn't make out which members of his staff had said what. He only felt gratitude that none of the three adults that remained of the once dozens of servants and staff of the Mondego estate hadn't run out of the door at the newest challenge of the collapsing estate.

A towel was handed to him, and he wiped his eyes. Blinking clear of the water, Zhi saw that Oswald, the butler, had opened a panel in the wall. The lights were restored as he pressed a black lever. Oswald's wife, Lin, carried in two empty buckets while her sister, Allana, plopped down a dry mop that was immediately dampened by the water at Zhi's feet.

He didn't have to command the skeletal staff that remained. They knew the drill. The estate had been in tatters for years.

"Thank you, Mathis," Zhi said handing back the towel to Oswald and Lin's young son.

Zhi rolled up his sleeves and started forward once more to see to the plumbing. His pedigree didn't lend to manual labor, but he'd had to learn these last few years. He'd learned to hang doors where all his life he'd had someone else open and close them for him. He'd learned to level tables and chairs where they'd always been set for him or pulled out for him to take a seat.

Luckily, his degree in music theory helped in this particular repair. Instead of a resonate clanging, the pipes made a gurgling sound. It was a clear indication that there was a clog.

"Snake," Zhi said.

Mathis handed over the device. Zhi went about the repairs as the thirteen-year-old pulled up a YouTube channel on how to fix the plumbing. On the screen, the capable looking female plumber slapped a wrench in the palm of her hand as she explained the finer points of the job.

Zhi found that women explained things in more detail than men did. Men typically just showed the steps with little to no instruction. Zhi had learned that lesson when he'd set about cleaning one of the fireplaces in the east wing and nearly burned the entire estate down.

He'd watched tons of videos to fix roofing, flooring, even videos on how to manage an estate. He certainly hadn't gotten proper tutelage from his father who'd been in charge of the estate before him.

The front of the Mondego estate was still gorgeous. The medieval towers and turrets were imposing in the early morning sky with the sun backlighting aged stones that made them glow copper. The stately home was bordered by woods and rocky hills so no one could see the travesty in the back.

Zhi worked hard to keep outward appearances up. This work was typically done under cover of night so that the neighbors wouldn't see. But inside the once majestic place, the facade was quickly crumbling. Many of the guest rooms weren't fit to keep pets in. The ballroom needed an entire facelift. The kitchens were outdated. The list went on.

When he was a kid, the Mondego estate was still majestic. It was because Zhi's grandfather, Hernán Díaz, had still been in charge. Once the old man passed on and the dukedom changed hands, the crumbling began.

Literally. The walls and plaster began to crumble. So had some of the flooring and a lot of the paint. But Zhi could only handle one thing at a time.

He shoved the snake farther and met with resistance. A few more shoves, a couple of twirls, and he was able to push the clog clear.

Zhi turned back to the gathered crowd with a look of triumph. Mathis held up his hand for a high five, which Zhi obliged with his free hand. The rest of the staff sighed with relief, shoulders dropping lower as though a burden had lifted. They were all about to disperse to tackle the next item on the day's list when the doorbell rang.

Zhi yanked the snake out in alarm. A gurgle of water gushed up, expelling some of the debris that had been trapped right in his face. The gunk slithered down his face and landed on his chest, right over his heart.

He had no time to recoil or sputter. "Places everyone."

Again, they knew the drill. Oswald dashed out of his work shirt and slipped on his service coat which always hung by the door for easy access. Lin dashed into the kitchen to put in a roll to make the place smell inviting and cover up the musky smell that permeated the walls. Allana and Mathis slipped out of sight.

Zhi dashed up to his bedroom. He stripped off his shirt and cargo pants. He ran a towel over his damp body, but too many water droplets clung. It would not do.

In the end, he slipped on swim trunks and a luxurious robe he'd taken from a hotel. He wouldn't dare step a pinky toe in the Olympic sized pool out back. He wasn't entirely convinced the Loch Ness monster hadn't taken up residence in that swamp.

Zhi made his way casually down the stairs, affecting the air he'd learned from his father. Before he moved forward, a shout sounded from above his head on the third floor. Zhi froze. He knew better than to step back. There was not much he could do but wait and pray the beast above wouldn't stir.

A small woman with dark, bone-straight hair and wide doe-like eyes materialized from a room. She looked delicate and frail dressed in a vibrantly red silk top with a Mandarin collar. She made brief eye contact with Zhi, and he saw the same slate gray eyes as his own looking back at him.

Wordlessly, a message was communicated from mother to son. Zhi nodded as his mother disappeared above the stairs to handle the monster while he went below to deal with the unexpected visitor.

By the time he reached the bottom stair, the grumbles from above ceased. Zhi let out a breath of relief. The beast was assuaged. For now.

Oswald appeared at the bottom of the stairs with a lanky gentleman who reminded Zhi of the nursery rhyme about Jack Sprat and his wife. This man was definitely portraying the role of the lean husband in the tale.

"A Mr. Schiessl to see you, Your Grace."

Zhi didn't know the name. But he didn't know many of the names of the people who stopped by the estate. His family no longer hosted parties on account of the former duke's condition. But they did receive visitors on account of the former duke's transgressions.

What would it be today? Gambling debts? Unpaid contracts? Or worse, another demand for a paternity test?

"I informed the gentleman that you were not at home to visitors." With his nose in the air as though he smelled something foul, Oswald did the perfect rendition of a snooty butler.

"I'm sorry, sir," said Mr. Schiessl, putting on a snooty air of his own. "But you'll have to see me. It's an urgent business matter."

"You will address him as *Your Grace*," Oswald snooted back.

"I'm not Cordovian," said Schiessl. The man sounded decidedly Eastern European. Perhaps Austrian?

"But I assume you have manners." Oswald glared at the intruder. A year ago, the butler would have never dared lose his temper. But these were trying times.

Zhi stepped in before the snooting turned to fisticuffs. "I was headed for a swim."

Oswald's gaze left their guests, and he rounded on Zhi in alarm.

With a quirk of his brow, Zhi assuaged the man of the notion that he would actually get into the diseased waters of the pool. "But I can spare a moment."

"I don't need a moment," said Schiessl, producing documents. "I'm here to serve you with papers."

Zhi recoiled from the documents. Watching his father, he knew better than to touch paperwork. Oswald took the offensive documents.

"As I'm sure you know, your father had many outstanding debts. A large number of them were with the Bank of Feldkirch in Austria."

Zhi knew of his father's debts here in Cordoba, and in Spain, and in England, and America. This was the first he was hearing about Austrian debts. Great. More to add to his ever-growing list of both repairs and debts that need repaying with ever dwindling funds.

"This debt was taken out five years ago. The

collateral was the estate. It must be paid in ninety days or the entire estate will be forfeited."

Zhi felt the blood stop in his body. It was as though Mr. Schiessl's words had clogged his entire system because nothing moved. There was already so much debt and very little income. There wasn't much in the coffers for a snake to move around and unclog.

Mr. Schiessl didn't bother to wait for a response. He turned on his skinny heel and headed back out the door. The staff materialized from the corners.

"We all knew this day would come," said Lin.

"I just hoped it wouldn't be in my lifetime," said Allana.

"But we'll rally," said Mathis. "You'll find a way. Won't you, Your Grace?"

The kid looked up at Zhi as though he hung the moon. Zhi felt like he was hanging from the moon by his fingertips. Just one more ray of light and he'd come crashing down.

He stared at the papers. He couldn't see how to fix this. He was sure there was no YouTube channel on how to go back in time and stop your father from swindling away an entire dukedom.

CHAPTER TWO

Spin watched the sea of people moving like waves. She was the moon pulling at the gravity of the large open space. With a flick of her wrists, the bodies slowed like a retreating wave pulling at the tide. With the slide of her fingers, she brought them back forward, arms straining overhead as they reached up toward the high ceiling. The crowd of warm bodies drenched in sweat inhaled as she held the needle over the vinyl record. Then she let the beat drop, and the bodies crashed into each other.

Being a DJ was life-bringing. She was heady off the power she commanded with just her hands and her ear for a good mix of beats. She looked out at the dance floor where she was the one making people feel, driving them into a frenzy, causing them to let loose their worries and woes and just be.

Spin cradled her headphones in one hand and

tweaked the faders with the other. Her own body bopped to the beat as the approaching change in tempo neared. This crowd got her. They felt the crescendo coming. They slowed their movements in anticipation. Spin could see the whites of their widened eyes as they held their breath.

She aligned the tempos, holding onto the notes, matching the beats before mixing in the new track. When she let the needle drop on the new song, the crowd went positively wild. Spin threw her hands in the air and jumped to the bass along with them.

As the sound came down, the applause drowned out the pulsing sound. Spin didn't take a bow. She never did after a session. It was the music and the muses that created this moment. It flowed through her as though God spoke to the crowd through her fingers.

Spin stepped off the stage and received accolades from the partygoers. She took them all in humbly, as her mother had taught her. People could always choose not to listen to the sounds she created, but they would always pay attention if she made them feel something.

Spin pressed her hand to her chest. The cool feel of the gem hanging on the chain reinforced the link to her mother. Spin knew the woman would be proud of her only daughter. If she were here.

"Great set, DJ Spin d'Elle."

"You set the roof on fire, girl."

Spin gave high fives. She accepted sweaty hugs.

She held out her hand for kandi when a girl slipped a few of the glowing bracelets over her wrist.

Even after her set, Spin was still on a high. She sipped at her cola, letting the sugar give her a rush. Who needed drugs when music could make you soar with zero side effects?

Though of course there were tipsy twits teetering in stilettos. Frat boys chugging beer after beer like it was Kool-Aide. And clueless stiffs dressed in what they thought was cool for a night slumming in a rave club.

Those types of partygoers annoyed Spin. They were here for an experience. Music was her life.

When a few of the frat boys made a beeline to her, Spin slipped behind the staging area. She was not into mama's boys. She had no desire to take care of anyone but herself, and those boys clearly advertised that they were looking for a girlfriend to do their laundry and beer runs. No, thank you.

Spin made quick work of the cables on the ground. She heard a thump and was sure one of her suitors had likely not been watching where he was going. Looking over her shoulder, she saw that she was home free. The way was clear.

"That was awesome."

Spin jumped, whipping around to face forward. A tiny brunette stood before her where the back hall had been empty a second before.

"Stop doing stuff like that, Lark." Spin huffed, her

heart rate pounding at its cage. "Keep your magic tricks on the stage where they belong."

"This is a stage."

Spin reached out and gave the woman a playful shove. Glitter flittered from Lark's shoulders like fairy dust. Spin looked at her friend quizzically.

Lark shrugged, casting more glitter from her person. "Part of the new act. The Great Nitwitini thinks it adds to the magic. More sparkle to razzle dazzle them."

"Well, at least he's stopped trying to saw you in half."

Lark rubbed at her belly and winced. That trick had not gone well during their practice sessions. The young magician never seemed able to get the hang of the oft-performed trick. Even Spin, who provided the music for their act, had been able to see through the illusion. As Nitwitini, or Northwood as his true surname was, grew increasingly frustrated, he also grew increasingly careless with the trick that included the use of a blade.

Lark had put her foot down about it. Luckily, it was while her legs were still attached to her body. As a magician's assistant, Lark had been put through the wringer. Literally.

"Are you sticking around here for the *after* after party?" Lark asked. "Or you headed out?"

Spin shook her head. "Nah, DJ Satisfriction is up next."

Both women cringed.

"All you had to say was the party is about to be over," said Lark.

DJ Satisfriction had a big bankroll, courtesy of his parents, and no skills. But he was a celebrity, so he brought in the crowd. Spin had warmed them up for him. Now he would cool them down, and the true partygoers would go off and find a new party. It was the Millennial way. They party hopped until dawn.

"Let's grab a bite," said Lark. "I'm starving. You're paying."

Before they could take two steps, Lark reached down and grabbed Spin's hand. She whirled on her friend with arched brows.

"You have gotten paid tonight, haven't you?"

Spin shrugged. She'd forgotten to go to the manager's office. She did this for the love, not the money. Before Spin could open her mouth, Lark steered them to the owner's office. Spin knew better than to protest the tiny bundle that was Lark Voorhees. She carried a wand and, unlike the magician she assisted, Lark knew how to use it.

The club manager looked up and grimaced when he saw Lark enter his office. No words were necessary. He didn't hesitate. Spin was certain the man didn't want a repeat of last week. Lark was just as good at making things disappear as she was at making them appear.

The manager reached in his desk drawer and drew

out a wad of cash. "I was just coming to find you, Spin. Here's your pay."

Lark snatched it and counted. The owner gritted his teeth as she did so. A drop of sweat trickled down his brow.

"It's one hundred Euros short," said Lark.

"What?" His brows rose in surprise. "It's what Spin and I agreed on. Right, Spin?"

It wasn't.

"Oh?" said Lark. "Well if you agreed to short her, I'm sure that money will appear someway somehow."

Lark turned back to the door, a mischievous grin on her face as she made her way to Spin.

"Wait," the manager called before Lark could cross the threshold.

The look on Lark's face screamed *thought so.*

He dove under his desk to the door to a hidden safe open that Spin had only learned was there after Lark's last visit with her to the office. Lark smirked when she saw his actions. She could get into it with no trouble. It wouldn't be the first time. He reemerged just a minute later with a fresh note.

Lark snatched it from his grubby hands with a polite smile that belied her true feelings. "Nice doing business with you."

"Lark," Spin tsked when they were out of the room, "You promised to use your powers for good."

"All bets are off when I'm hungry. Besides, he's a chauvinist. He pays the male DJs more than you. He's lucky I didn't change the combination of his safe after emptying it."

"It has a lock and key now."

"Child's play." Lark handed Spin the wad of cash as they exited into the warehouse that had been converted into a club.

Most of the places Spin played were such converted places. A cool breeze greeted them as they stepped outside the sweat-drenched club and into the night air of Nice, France. Being near the water, the nights always turned a bit cold. As the two friends began to go down the list of possible places there was to eat, a rustling sound came from behind the garbage can.

They froze. But they saw a gruff shoe poking out from behind the overflowing dumpster. It was a woman. Her face was covered in smudges of dirt. She clutched a half-eaten sandwich in one hand. She held onto the similarly grubby hand of a child in the other.

The child was a bit cleaner with somewhat nicer clothes. She held a burger patty with no bread. She chewed quickly as she eyed Lark and Spin, as though she was afraid they'd take her last bite of food away.

Spin took careful, slow steps as she went over to them. The mother pushed the child behind her. Spin peeled off the one hundred Euro note and handed it to the mother. The woman's eyes grew wide.

Without waiting for a thanks or any praise, Spin turned and continued on her way with Lark in tow.

She didn't hear anything from her friend. They'd both known that particular struggle.

"Thanks for getting me all that I was due," Spin said. "You were right, I needed it."

Spin pressed her hand to her heart, finding all the security she needed in the cold gem she found there. She knew money was necessary. But holding on to it only brought bad things. Money behaved best when it was put into service for someone in need.

CHAPTER THREE

The office looked as though a tornado had passed through and took a bird bath. Papers were everywhere. File drawers were opened and gutted. Shelves were divulged of books. Still, in the chaos, Zhi had found nothing to save them. There was no path to turn around what his father had torn asunder. For years, Zhi had tried to put the estate back together piece by piece, dollar by dollar, stone by stone.

When he was younger, he lived oblivious to the chaos his father created. He'd been in the calm of the eye, left to run wild with Prince Alex and Carlisle, the son of the Baron of Balansya. Being born the son of nobility, each of the boys had rarely seen their patrons. The king, duke, and baron had preferred their boys be out of sight, which had been fine for the boys, none of which had ever lived up to their old man's expectations.

Zhi had stayed out of sight but not so far that he hadn't known of his father's temper and tantrums. He knew his father hadn't always come home at night. He never saw or heard his mother cry, but he knew that she did. She would always cover her sobs with one of Chopin's nocturnes.

Zhi had set his path in life to be nothing like his father. He never raised his voice. He never drank more than one glass of spirits even when at home. He only gambled on silly wagers like foot races between his friends and pie contests with the prince.

He had his fun but at no one else's expense. He'd never made a woman cry. He'd never put anyone out of work. That would all change very soon. The house would be empty of staff if he didn't find a solution. The halls would only echo with the sad chords from his mother's fingers as she covered her sobs with a sad serenade in D major.

Zhi slumped in the ornate chair. The decades' old upholstery coughed up dusk as his head collided with the wingback fabric. The dust burned his eyes, but no moisture leaked from them. He was his mother's son. He might have to visit the music room himself later this evening for his own pity party.

Nian Zhen, the duchess of Mondego, came into the room on silent feet. The ancient door didn't dare creak at her presence. The floorboards hushed under her slight weight. The only reason Zhi knew his mother was there was because of the ruffle of the papers at her feet.

She looked down at the discarded heap of parchment. It was another of her husband's messes. So, of course, she thought it her duty to take care of it. Even at the age of fifty, Nian sank gracefully down to her knees and began tidying up.

"Stop that," Zhi shouted. His voice was harsh, and she flinched. Zhi felt like the dregs in the pool out back. But he was brimming with disgust like those foul waters. "It's not your mess to clean up."

"It's not yours either."

His mother's voice was so soft. It always had been. He'd never once heard her raise it in all his life.

Not when her husband berated her after her wealthy family cut off his access to their accounts. Not when Diego Sr. came home after days—weeks—of being absent with another woman's perfume on his jacket. Not even when fists were slammed into walls when they were alone behind closed doors.

Zhi wasn't sure if any of those jabs connected with his mother's flesh. If they did, Nian hid them well. Their one-sided arguments could be heard from any wing in the house. But the former duke never put his bad behavior on full display.

In all his years, those were the first critical words his mother had ever said against her husband. Zhi rose slowly from his chair. The dust held its breath as he did so. He crossed the room in two strides to come to his mother's side.

"I can't fix this, *mǔqīn*," he said, using the formal Chinese word for mother.

Though his mother grew up in Spain, the daughter of first-generation immigrants to the country, his grandparents still held to many of the old ways.

"There is nothing left," he said, taking the papers from her delicate hands. "He's lost it all. No one will loan a peso or pence or a cent to anyone with the name of Mondego."

"You can't ask your friends to intervene?"

His mother's eyes remained downcast as she said the words. That's how Zhi knew it wasn't her idea. The monster had whispered the notion in her ear, pulling at her strings like a devil sitting beside her on the piano bench.

Zhi knew she meant Alex, the Prince of Cordoba. Or maybe she'd been referring to the king himself. There were only a few years of difference between Zhi and King Leonidas. With Zhi being a constant at Alex's side, the king and the son of a duke had also forged a bond.

But Zhi shook his head. He couldn't ask his friends to clean up his father's mess. They all were living in the shadows of the men who'd sired them. Leo was far too busy with reigning the country away from economic crisis. Alex was trying to make his own way with a business venture. Carlisle was steering the ship of the barony while his father clutched on to life and the illusion of power.

The writing on the wall was clear since it wasn't on any of the papers in the duke's office. Zhi would have to get a job. But doing what? His degree was in music theory. It was a degree he'd never expected to use as his life would be spent running the estate.

He had his mother's talent, but like her, he had never played professionally. Only in the music room to pound out his feelings or to please her. How was he going to support his mother?

And then there was the staff. He couldn't think of where they'd go. Like Zhi, the three adults that remained from the once sizable workforce had each been there all their lives. Their parents had worked for the dukedom for generations. Zhi had watched young Mathis toddle around these halls. He'd played catch with the boy while his father tended to his duties. The staff was more family to him than his own father.

This was one man's fault. That man was resting comfortably while the rest of them suffered due to his actions. Zhi's gaze fixed on the ceiling as though he could beam a laser up to the third floor and burn his father into oblivion.

"How is he? Is he lucid today?"

His mother swallowed before answering. "He is calm. Let's keep him that way."

Nian rested a hand on her son's shoulder. That was his mother's way. She never rocked the boat. She did her duty, what was expected of her. And she never complained.

Well, Zhi had enough of his father's blood in him to launch a complaint. Ignoring his mother's gentle rebuke, Zhi left the office and took the stairs. Coming up to the highest level of the estate, he approached his father's room.

The room was bare. Not out of spite for the once large and powerful man. It was because even in his weakened form, he could still wreak havoc with anything in reach of his throwing arm.

Diego Ferdinand Constantine Mondego loomed like a shadow in the large bed. He'd once been broad and imposing. Now he was meek and frail. His once tan skin was white and delicate like porcelain. He'd come from Spanish conquistadors. He now looked like something a fisherman's net had snagged.

The man was dying. Slowly, painfully, and dragging the estate and everyone in it with him on his descent into hell. For the last three years, he was no longer mentally capable of performing his ducal duties, and the reins had been handed over to his only son.

The feeble old man opened his eyes, the pupils unfocused for a moment but quickly found Zhi. Zhi held his breath and froze on the threshold. Sometimes, the former duke didn't even recognize his own son. It was worse when he did.

"Oh, it's you," Diego snarled. Though his body had

lost might, his voice hadn't. The low grumble of a lion filled the room. But the man in the bed was no match for a starved alley cat. "What do you want?"

"More solicitors came. Something about a loan in Austria."

Diego rolled his eyes. Zhi wasn't sure if it was from his illness or annoyance.

"Because you put the estate up as collateral for a debt you knew you couldn't pay; they have the right to take the estate unless I can pay off the monies you owe. The problem is, there is no money left and nothing incoming."

"Insolent brat," the old man spat. "You do understand that money does, in fact, grow on trees. Your mother's people make enough of it with their little cleaning service."

Zhi winced at the insult. His mother's family had become self-made millionaires with a chain of convenience stores and laundromats throughout Spain. But they had two strikes against them; they were nouveau riche, and they were immigrants. Two things the ancient and noble blood of the Mondegos turned their aquiline noses up at.

But when millions turned to billions, Diego held his nose and wooed the shy and sheltered daughter of those same wealthy immigrants. Nian's father was suspicious, but it mattered not. His daughter had fallen desperately in love, and in love, she stayed, even after Diego showed his true colors after spending every bit of her inheritance.

"If your mother's family would give me the money they promised—"

"My mother is not a commodity," said Zhi. "You at least could show remorse since you won't and can't take responsibility for all the pain you've caused."

"There's a simple enough solution to this problem." His father's eyes were bright and lucid as they focused on Zhi. "Marry more money."

Zhi tried to swallow the bile that rose in his throat. He failed. His father had learned nothing. He would never change.

"Find an ugly, rich heiress and seduce her out of her pocketbook. It's what nobles have been doing for generations. It is your sole job in your capacity as a duke."

"You disgust me."

"I kept you fed and in the lap of luxury all your life," his father roared. What was left of the old lion in him reared its head. "You weren't disgusted while you were reaping the fruits of my labors."

Zhi couldn't stomach another moment around the man. He slammed the door and left him to his rages. A few moments later, Zhi heard the quiet snick of the door and the silence that told him his father had calmed down. Zhi knew his mother had gone in and tended to the man she loved despite everything he'd done to her.

CHAPTER FOUR

"And now you say the magic words ..."

"Abracadabra!"

Spin couldn't help but grin as the adolescents' shouts sounded all throughout the small theater. After their enthusiastic cheers, Spin added the drum roll sound effect to the cacophony. From her place just off the stage behind the curtains, she turned back to the main event.

The Great Piers Northwood, Illusionist Extraordinaire, waved his perfectly manicured slender fingers over a pristine top hat. The stage lighting caught the sparkles of the eye shadow he'd placed over his eyelids. His thin lips gleamed from the second coat of gloss Spin had watched him apply before the show.

Of course, The Great Nitwitini wasn't holding the hat. That job was reserved for his faithful assistant. Spin's gaze traveled to Lark whose knuckles were white as she gripped the hat. Her ruby red smile was forced. Her pale eyes shot daggers at her boss as she passed in a skimpy costume that wasn't wholly appropriate for the age group in the audience. But The Great Nitwitini insisted it was the look he wanted for his show.

Nitwitini waved his hands again and slotted her a meaningful glance. Lark let out a huffed breath. Glitter shimmied off her shoulders with the action. Taking the hat from her, Nitwitini turned the prop upside down.

Nothing came out.

The children leaned forward in their seats trying to see if there was anything to see. The rabbit that was supposed to jump out was nowhere to be seen. The silence was deafening.

Nitwitini's smile faltered before the peering crowd of children. He nervously chuckled. "I don't think I heard you. Say the magic words again. Louder this time so Mr. Rabbit can hear you."

The kids enthusiastically obliged. Once more, they shouted the age-old magical word. From behind the curtain, Spin played the drum roll again.

The Great Nitwitini gave his back to the children as he began his hand waving motions. He glared at Lark as he did so. Her smile was genuine this time. Spin knew her friend was enjoying the performance.

Finally, after all the fanfare, Nitwitini once more took the hat from his assistant. He turned over the hat.

Nothing.

Nitwitini looked panicked. Lark's gaze was innocent as she shrugged. More of the hated sparkles shimmered down from her shoulders. From her place off stage, Spin cringed. She had no idea what her friend had planned, but unlike the magician, Spin knew better than to cross the one person on the stage who actually held all the cards.

The kids in the audience began to murmur. Then their little bodies began to fidget in their seats. A small giggle broke through the murmuring. Followed by a few chuckles. Then the pointing started, and all the children broke out laughing.

The hat was still in Lark's hands. On her shoulder, sniffing at the hated sparkles, was Mr. Rabbit. Lark dropped the hat to snuggle the white rabbit in her arms.

Nitwitini glared, his face going red.

Lark stepped in front of him and spread her bountiful arms wide and shouted "Ta-dah."

The children sprang to their feet, clapping vigorously. It took Nitwitini a second to get in line with the new reality. They all thought it was a part of the act. He quickly relieved Lark of the bunny, stepped in front of her, and took a bow, accepting the praise and the credit as though it were his.

"One of these days, you're going to play a trick that your mouth can't cash," said Spin.

"He deserved it," Lark said. "There's glitter in my bra."

Lark held up the wash towel she'd been using for the better part of fifteen minutes. The once white cloth had turned a bright shade of gold. She tossed the ruined towel in the trash bin, and the two women headed out the back of the old theater.

The afternoon air was warm as they rounded the old building. A few kids were still outside the theater surrounding Nitwitini. They didn't look up at Lark's approach. No one was interested in the magician's assistant. Even though the assistants performed most of the work that created the illusions while the magicians distracted the audience.

"You need your own show," said Spin.

Lark didn't disagree. Instead, she asked a rhetorical question. "How many female magicians can you name?"

She knew Spin had no real answer. Not many people outside the magic industry did. Outside of that actress in that Hollywood movie about magic, Spin couldn't name one, even though Lark had rattled off a few names which Spin had promptly forgotten.

"But I'll tell you this," Lark said looping her arm through Spin's, "I am tired of pulling weight for men."

"Amen to that, sister."

It was the same in the music industry. Men held most of the power be they producers, promoters, artists, or DJs. The entertainment industry was tough for those of the female persuasion.

"You could go back to dancing," Spin offered as they turned the corner that would take them to their street.

It was another rhetorical statement which didn't warrant a real response. Spin knew her friend had been bitten by the magic bug. Lark was in it for life. Her dancer's body was what got her jobs with magicians who wanted to stuff her in small places, slice her in half, and use her looks to distract the audience. The problem was that Lark was more talented than each man she'd ever assisted.

"I just need someone to see my talent and want me alone on a stage," Lark said. "Not as a sidekick."

"Well, you're my heroine."

"Ahhhh." Lark pressed a fierce kiss onto Spin's cheek. "Love you too, girl."

Lark was the first real friend Spin had had in a long time. Both girls were American transplants in a foreign land. Well, Spin was only partly American. But it was the part she claimed. The other half of her didn't exist as far as she was concerned.

"You need a break of your own," Lark said, changing the subject. "Don't you want to be on the big stage? To sell out crowds like Paris Hilton?"

"How dare you." Spin came to an abrupt halt, making Lark stumble. Good. She deserved it for that tasteless crack.

Lark chuckled at Spin's reaction to being compared to the socialite turned DJ. One night the two women had gone to one of the heiress' shows, preparing to heckle and make fun. They both had been shocked when they found themselves having a good time and vibing to the tracks the Manhattan debutante mixed. Lark had never let Spin live that night down.

"I don't need a big stage," said Spin. "Small clubs and secret raves are all I want."

She had no desire to make a name for herself. Since the name she was currently using wasn't her real one. She didn't want those who knew her true identity to ever find her.

The two women crossed the street to arrive at the hostel they both were staying at. The building had never seen better days. Spin was sure it had been designed with crumbling brick and rusted metal. But it was cheaper than renting a flat. And it came furnished with everything they needed; a bed and a closet.

"You coming out tonight to the rave?"

"Yeah," said Lark. "I just need a disco nap if I'm gonna roll with you all night and into the dawn."

"See you in a few hours, sleeping beauty. I'm gonna grab something from the shop before heading up."

Lark slipped into the back door while Spin circled around front. She was looking forward to tonight's party. She was looking forward to showing off the new beats she'd been playing around with earlier in the day.

Spin liked to push the boundaries and mix old tracks from the eighties and nineties with new hits from today. She liked crossing musical genre lines and sneak in a country ballad with hip hop. She joyed in fusing a classical piano riff with an electronic beat.

"Her name is Eleanor Trent."

Spin froze in place. She took a step back and pressed her form into the crumbling brick at the side of the building. She was just under the manager's office. The cheapskate had the windows thrown wide open because air conditioner wasn't a word in his vocabulary.

"You know anybody by that name?"

Spin didn't recognize the voice of the speaker. But she did recognize the accent. The man was Austrian.

"Never heard of her," said the owner.

Slowly, carefully, Spin inched her body up to peer into the window. Standing on her tiptoes, she got a good look at the Austrian man. He was tall and thin as a crepe. She didn't recognize him. She didn't need to. She knew what he was looking for.

Spin pressed her hand to her heart. When the cold gem made contact with her skin, she felt a second of relief. But only a second. She would not let this man find what he sought.

"But you don't need a birth certificate or

identification to rent here," the owner was saying. "Just cash."

The crepe-shaped man pursed his lips. He looked left and right. Spin ducked down, pressing herself against the building. A few seconds later, she saw him crossing the street to the next hostel. He'd get the same reaction from them. No one here knew the name he'd used because she never used it. Still, her heart beat fast to know that she'd have to leave soon.

CHAPTER FIVE

"Y ou want to have your stag party where?" Carlisle scratched at the blond curls atop his head. His green gaze went from Zhi to Alex and back again, hazy with incomprehension.

"In my restaurant." Alex spread his arms around the inside of the Prince's Palate. His usual mischievous grin was filled with pride of ownership as his dark eyes surveyed his small kingdom.

The three friends sat at the bar which was pushed up to the kitchen where they had a front-row seat of the food preparation going on behind the scenes. The restaurant wasn't technically open to the public, there were still renovations going on in the main dining area. But Alex and his fiancée had a tasting for some movers and shakers in the culinary world happening in just a matter of days. So, being the true friends that they were, Zhi and Carlisle had volunteered to be taste testers.

"We'll close shop for the night," Alex continued, "and I'll fly in chefs from around the world. We can even make it a culinary competition like that show where the chefs cook head to head."

The man was beaming at his idea of a bachelor party fit for a prince. Both Zhi and Carlisle gawked at their friend. Silently, Zhi let out a relieved sigh. He'd expected Alex would want a destination party on some private island. Zhi couldn't afford to take that particular duty on as his best man. He could barely afford lunch.

Thankfully, this bill was being covered by Alex as the owner. It was the best meal Zhi had had in months, mainly because the last sumptuous bite of food he'd had had been prepared by Alex's fiancée, Jan, when she'd won the annual Union Day pie making competition. He'd dreamed about that slice of pie ever since.

Jan emerged from the kitchens with a dish. The pretty blonde rattled off a list of exotic ingredients that were in the dish which Zhi promptly tuned out. His ears were far too full of the scents wafting in the air, and his tongue only cared about sampling the fare.

Zhi and Carlisle groaned with delight as the first morsel hit their tongues. Meanwhile, Alex had interrupted the pie maker with a kiss before she could escape the table.

"I know what I'm having for dessert," he said into her ear, but loud enough for the carpenters in the other room to hear his claim.

"My potatoes are gonna burn." Jan gave him a playful shove and then dashed out of his way before he could grab her again.

Alex beamed after the woman. Zhi had never seen his friend look adoringly at any woman except his niece, Penelope. Other than Penelope or his brother's soon to be wife, Esme, Zhi had never seen Alex actually look a woman in the eye.

They all had had their fair share of partying. But now Alex was settling down. He was not only the happiest Zhi had ever seen him, but he also looked content with his lot in life.

The prince was marrying for love. Not title. Not money. Though that's what everyone had initially assumed. But love was clear in both the prince and the pie maker's eyes.

Zhi had seen the same look in King Leo's eyes. Leo had married for duty his first go around. He hadn't been unhappy. But with his second wife, Esme, he had the same sparkle as his brother.

Love matches were rare for nobles. Even in this day and age. From somewhere in the back of his mind, he swore he heard his father snort at the idea. The delectable bite of food on his tongue turned bitter with the memory of his father's words from earlier.

Marry more money.

Zhi set his fork down. He picked up his folded linen and pressed it against his mouth, trying to clear the distasteful thought from his palate.

He hadn't planned to marry for love. Sure, he'd figured he'd marry someone from his own class, someone who he found compatible on things that mattered. They'd have some things in common, like music or art. But he couldn't imagine deceiving a woman as his father had done his mother.

Zhi had seduced his fair share of women. But they all came to him willingly. He made no promises. Most enjoyed the novelty of landing a duke, even if only for a short period.

He wondered if anyone would ever date him now that he was about to be destitute? Looking up, he saw Alex and Carlisle laughing. He knew the two had their own burdens, but money wasn't one of them. Would his friends be there for him when he became penniless?

He knew they would. They'd been through enough that money, or the lack thereof, would not rip them apart. They'd likely want to help him, to at least give him shelter.

It wasn't himself he was worried about. It was mainly his mother's reaction to impending poverty that concerned him.

Nian Zhen had been raised in luxury back in Spain. But she'd also been scorned because of her heritage and the newness of her family's money. It had made her shy and reserved. He also suspected it was a major contributing factor in why she accepted the abuse her husband doled out to her over the years. She never felt that she belonged, not to his society, not to his world.

She rarely made public appearances. Which had been perfectly fine in her husband's eyes. It was easier for him to carry on his affairs without his golden ball and chain standing beside him. Mondego House had become as much her cell as it was her home. Zhi wasn't sure she would survive outside its walls.

She'd been turned out by her family after choosing and then sticking with her husband. She'd had her heart broken by the man she thought would love and protect her for always. Through it all, she'd never said an ill word about any of the people who were meant to care for her but had trudged over her. She deserved better.

"She deserves the world," Alex was saying. His gaze was on Jan's figure in the kitchen window as she stood over a stove. "Can you believe her ex left her at the altar? Literally. He just left her there and walked away. I can't imagine ever being away from that woman for the length of time it takes to bake a casserole."

"Afraid she'll run?" said Carlisle.

Alex threw a buttered roll at him which Carlisle caught and took a bite out of.

Zhi couldn't imagine feeling that way about a

woman. He felt that way about his mother, his home, even his staff. He loved the place and the people who'd been there his whole life.

"When you find the person you want to spend the rest of your life with," said Alex, "you want to give them everything."

"Never thought I'd see the day when the Playboy Prince would settle down," said Carlisle.

"You know all those stories in the papers were false," said Alex.

"Not all of them," Zhi corrected. "Don't forget, we know you."

"Is this wedding planning with the bride's maids?"

The three men at the bar all turned to see Omar, the Marquis of Navarre coming up behind them. The man moved like he was the king of the desert. His dark gaze assessed the situation with amusement and clarity.

"You ladies deciding on flowers for your bouquets?" Omar said as he clasped each of their hands in turn.

"You'll help with entertainment," said Alex. It wasn't a question. But neither was it a command. They all simply knew what the marquis' response would be.

"I practically raised you," Omar said. "Of course, I'll help with your little hen party."

Omar was only a few years older than the three of them. He, Leo, and the Earl of Larida were a threesome much like Zhi, Alex, and Carlisle.

"We can get started once I'm back." Omar plopped down on a stool and picked up Zhi's fork. "I'm headed to France to sail back to Cordoba on a cruise ship."

"Lifestyles of the rich and famous," chided Zhi as the entertainment producer gorged himself on the scraps left on Zhi's plate.

"Rich, yes. Famous, not so much. I was invited by a tech billionairesse. Parker Paley-Li, have you heard of her?"

Omar laid a magazine down on the bar. It opened to a paper clipped page. On the glossy spread, Zhi saw a grimacing female.

This Parker Paley-Li might have been smiling, but there was a tug at the corner of her mouth that pointed down. Her hair was a riot of colors, and the glasses she wore over her eyes reminded Zhi of someone from the fifties.

"She's doing amazing things with coding and computers," said Omar, around the last bite off Zhi's plate. He reached over for Carlisle's plate, but his advance was met with a threatening butter knife.

Zhi paid no attention to the food war. His attention was riveted to the words beneath the tech pioneer's photograph.

In the article, the reporter asked Parker about her love life. She said she was sadly single but looking. She went on to say that she didn't have any game. She lamented how potential partners found her brains and her money intimidating, so she hadn't found that special someone.

"You're staring pretty hard there, Your Grace," said Carlisle.

Zhi's head shot up from the magazine. He wasn't one to blush, but he felt his cheeks redden. He had no idea why? He wasn't thinking any impure thoughts about the girl.

Marry more money.

"Don't tell me you're looking to get off the market too?" Carlisle's face turned horror-stricken. "Don't leave me alone out here."

Zhi shrugged, then shoved the magazine from him. "Her story is interesting is all."

"She is interesting," said Omar. "Her father immigrated to the States after college and rose up in the ranks of Silicon Valley. She took his knowledge and passion for computers and built herself an empire at the ripe age of twenty-two. She also loves music. You two have a lot in common. You should come with me."

Marry more money.

"I can't."

The fork paused halfway to Omar's mouth. Zhi may have said those two words a bit more forcefully than he'd meant to. But it was because he'd been answering the voice in his head and not that of his friend.

"I can't," Zhi repeated and a more socially acceptable volume. "I have responsibilities at home."

"How is your father?" asked Alex.

"Same as always," said Zhi. "Making everyone around him miserable on his descent into hell."

"Sorry," said Carlisle.

Zhi knew the man sympathized. His father was the same in almost every way. Though Carlisle had managed to step in and save his inheritance before things got dire. No one knew how bad things were for the Mondego estate. And Zhi wasn't about to tell.

"You should come and take a break," said Omar. "It's just an overnight trip. Parker is rewarding her entire staff with a weekend cruise to our humble homeland. She's rented out my club for the weekend, too. Come let your hair down before it gets pinned up with planning this wedding."

Zhi looked again at the magazine. He thumbed it open to the page of Parker's interview. Further down in the spread, the reporter asked if Parker was looking for a prince charming or a titan of industry. Parker's answer was neither. She was looking for a person who was compatible. They had to love music, be devoted to their mom, like she was, and not be afraid to get their hands dirty when times got rough.

"What do you say?" asked Omar.

The lump in Zhi's throat was a little hard to swallow, but he managed. "A little weekend getaway might be just what I need."

CHAPTER SIX

The lights flared over the ceiling, across the floor, and around the room. The crowd threw their hands up in the air, fingers splayed open as people jumped. It looked like fireworks of the flesh to Spin. She closed her eyes, not needing to see what her own hands were doing. She worked the turntables as though they were her magic trick, and she made each and every one of the people gathered disappear inside her hat, tumbling down into the depths of the beat to escape whatever they were running from.

The party was just getting started at one in the morning, and the fashionably late had yet to arrive. Spin went through her playlist. It was a multigenerational, multi-genre mash up. She layered Funkadelic with Nirvana, Motown divas with pulsing electronica, classic elevator music with jazz.

Music was music, and she hated labels. If the beats

lined up, she'd toss them into the mix and watch the crowd go wild. They were near to stampeding as she layered in a nursery rhyme over a thumping House beat. Spin stomped her feet to the beat and clapped her hands in time to the impish lyrics right along with them. After her close call earlier in the day, she needed to get lost.

Music had been her escape all her life. When Spin was a child, her mother, Angelica, had taught her about chords and individual notes and music. Angelica would play the part of the flute. Spin remembered listening to the light, airy notes, chasing after them as they swirled around in her imagination.

Playing the same song, her mother strummed the notes on an acoustic guitar. Angelica's nimble fingers tickled the keys, shimmying over Spin's shoulder and making her want to shake her body in time to the music.

Her mother would later sit at the piano or behind a drum set or stand and strum the violin. Angelica was a prodigy who played every instrument. Spin would twirl and dance to each layer, understanding their solo story as well as how each chapter of the songbook went together making a cacophony of harmony.

Spin could pick out each instrument as well as hear them together. She'd closed her eyes and get lost in the melodic ease of the piano. She'd sail away on the notes of the violin. She'd escape behind the pulsing drumbeats. Listening to the music now always brought her closer to her mother. As close as she could get now that they would forever be out of each other's reach.

Spin opened her eyes to the flashing lights and fists punching in the air. Her heart raced as she looked out over the crowd. Not a single face was recognizable, just the feeling that she was being watched, and she'd need to run.

She sped up the tempo until she felt her heart would burst. She'd have to run again. She'd have to slip into the roar of the world until she blended into the pulse of a crowd and couldn't be distinguished from one note to the next.

With her time on stage nearing its completion, Spin brought the music to a dénouement. She lifted the needle on the turntables. The silence lasted a split second before the crowd went wild.

"Spin d'Elle," they chanted.

She didn't bow. She lifted her hands and pointed out to the crowd, thanking the people for taking the journey with her. Now she had to leave them for a journey of her own. By morning, she'd step onto a new land, find new chords and melodies to mix together a new story.

She was never alone as long as she had her music. There was nowhere that she'd ever called home. She and her mother had moved since Spin had started to walk. She remembered seeing the roots of a tree and asking her mother what the gnarled, spindly thing was. Even as a child, she couldn't fathom how something could burrow into the ground and stay, never leaving the one spot.

Houses were temporary. She'd never owned a dresser where she'd put away clothes. A suitcase was the only storage she needed. She had hers backstage. In it was all she needed.

Over the year she'd been in Nice, Spin had never acquired more than would fit inside the case. There had been too many times in her youth when her mother would tell her they had to go and Spin would agonize over leaving something that wouldn't fit in her small Hannah Montana suitcase behind.

She'd learned her lesson well.

Spin looked around as she stepped off the raised platform. She doubted she'd see the tall, crepe-thin man in the makeshift club. Raves were a thing that began in the Generation X days. The man who'd been snooping around her hostel looked as though he could've been born at the start of that generation. But he didn't look like he was the type that had spun glow sticks in his youth.

She collected her thumb drive. All her music fit inside the small digital device. The clubs all had their own setup. She simply needed to plug in and play. She could do that wherever she was in the world.

There would be more auditioning and proving herself in the next place she landed. But it was her only option. She couldn't stay here and be found.

Where would she go this time? Maybe she should go back to America. But it was too risky. Too many people still remembered her mom.

Hiding in plain sight had been her strategy for a bit. It had worked for a while as she bounced around Europe. But now the jig was up.

She'd hadn't been to Asia or the Middle East. New adventures, new music, new parties. Whichever fare was cheaper, that's where she'd go.

Decision made, she headed back to the manager's office to collect her pay for the night. Now was the time she wished Lark was at her side. Her only friend was probably out in the crowd dancing her sparkles away, but Spin was doing her best to avoid her friend. She hated goodbyes.

"So, where to next?"

Spin pulled up short, nearly jumping out of her skin. The hall had been empty before. Now Lark stood there.

"For crying out loud." Spin clutched at her heart from the fright.

"Sorry, sorry," Lark giggled. "I won't do it again. I promise."

Lark held up her fingers in what she'd told Spin was the Girl Scout pledge. Spin wouldn't know. She'd never stayed anywhere long enough to memorize a pledge.

"You on your way to get paid?" Lark looped her arm through Spin's and leaned her head on her shoulder. "'Cause I'm starved. Let's pool our money and go someplace nice tonight."

Spin sighed, relaxing into her friend's hold. It wouldn't hurt to wait until dawn to leave. She wouldn't tell Lark she was going. This would be the last night they had together. She'd make it memorable.

"That was a fantastic set," said a husky voice from behind them.

Spin looked the newcomer up and down. The young woman had multicolored hair -every shade of the rainbow. Either she had a deft hand when it came to hair dye or that had cost a pretty penny at the salon. Her prescriptive glasses were wing-tipped like something from the movie *Grease*. Spin liked the mashup.

"Thanks." Spin gave the girl a head nod.

"The way you mixed the seventies music with today's. And then you tossed in a classical riff? My heart is still pounding from it."

Yeah, this girl got it. "Thanks ..." Spin waited for the woman to fill in her name.

"I'm Parker."

"Spin."

"I know." Parker grinned, but not in the cheesy fangirl way. It was in a way that showed awe and respect for Spin's talent. "Listen, I know it's short notice, but if you're at all free tomorrow, I'd love for you to DJ my office party."

Spin hesitated. She wasn't trying to stay in Nice for any longer than necessary.

"But there's a catch," Parker continued. "It's not here in France. It's on a cruise ship."

"An office party on a cruise ship?"

"Yeah, it's a business thing. A retreat for all the workers."

"You have a cool boss."

Parker shrugged. "Some think so. So, are you in? I happen to know the boss is very generous when it comes to entertainment. Plus, a free cruise. And your friend is welcome to come along."

Lark tugged at Spin's arm like she was a kid being offered her pick on the ice cream truck. Her eyes went puppy dog wide as she silently pleaded.

"Where are you sailing?" asked Spin.

"A small island in the Mediterranean Sea. It's called Cordoba."

That was even closer to the Middle East than France. Her fare would likely be cut in half from the island. What did Spin have to lose? It would get her out of France for free, give her some more time with Lark, and she'd get a paycheck out of it.

CHAPTER SEVEN

It was the height of wastefulness. Flying two hours to France to sail for ten hours back to Córdoba. Zhi would've done it without a second thought a few years back when he didn't know the balance of his family's accounts. Now, his belly ached at the expense, even though it wasn't his dime being spent.

Stepping off Omar's private jet into the bright Nice afternoon, Zhi let out a long, weary sigh. What was he doing here? He had no time for such frivolous activities as an overnight cruise. His to-do list back at Mondego House was ever increasing.

He wouldn't be wrong to say the list was taking on water. The estate was sinking. The booty had been looted, the coffers ransacked. He and his staff were all standing on a shaky plank. The smart thing would be to jump ship, not board someone else's ship. But that's what he was doing.

He stepped onto the cruise liner hired out by the tech billionairesse. There was no red carpet. Instead, it was neon pink and yellow with glowing painted arrows directing traffic. Partially clad bodies, some also in glowing neon, roamed the main deck in trunks and two-piece swimsuits. The aesthetic was beach resort meets warehouse party with a pool at the center of the party, deck chairs fanning out, and a massive dance floor with bodies moving and gyrating.

There couldn't be more than one hundred people on board the massive ocean liner that easily carried five thousand or more. Zhi was noticing more and more how the rich flushed money down the toilet. Probably because he knew how to fix toilets now.

"Omar, you made it." A tall, thin woman in cargo pants stepped out of the crowd with her arms wide. The rainbow colored hair announced that she was the event's hostess and the woman whose interest Zhi hoped to garner.

"Parker." Omar embraced the young woman. She was engulfed in the massive arms of his friend. After the hugs and pleasantries, Omar turned to Zhi. "Parker, allow me to introduce my dear friend, Diego Zhi Wen de Bernadino, the Duke of Mondego."

"Wow, that's a mouthful." Parker grinned.

Instead of an open-armed hug, she stuck out her hand. Sideways with her fingers splayed, not palms

down in preparation for kissed knuckles. When Zhi
went to turn her knuckles up for the more noble
greeting, she clasped his fingers in a firm handshake.
Undaunted, Zhi turned her palm down and brushed
his lips over her knuckles. When he looked up, she
had one brow raised and the other lowered in a
quizzical look.

"Europeans," Parker chuckled. She grinned good-
naturedly and patted Zhi's hand.

The gesture reminded Zhi of how his mother used
to pat his hand or his cheek when he'd done
something to make her proud of him.

Zhi released her hand. Maternal pride wasn't the
direction he was aiming for with this woman. At this
rate, he was headed right into the friend zone. Or
possibly worse, the little kiddie zone.

He straightened to his full height. But found that
he only had about half an inch on Parker. She was tall
and wearing flats.

"Let me get some kandi for you both." Parker dug
into the shoulder bag resting on her hip.

Zhi took a deep breath and clenched his teeth. He
knew Parker was into the rave scene from reading the
article, and a few other articles he'd found about her
on Google. He'd never been one for the drug scene. He
could never be with a woman who casually did drugs.

He frowned as he watched Parker slide colorful
neon bracelets over Omar's wrist. She turned to Zhi
holding a few more of the strung beads. He wondered

if they were perhaps edible? But as she slid them over his wrist, he could tell they were nothing but plastic.

"Why don't you two go put your bags down," she said. "The party's about to get started."

The party hadn't started yet? There was loud music playing, bodies swaying, and drinks flowing. He began to wonder even more what he had gotten himself into. Parker gave Omar another huge grin and shoulder squeeze, then she turned to greet the next set of guests to come aboard.

Zhi watched after her for a moment. She wasn't the type of girl he typically dated. She was in cargo pants and a graphic T-shirt. Dark eyeliner lit her brow, and only a coat of lip gloss touched her lips.

She hadn't given him the googly-eyed gaze he was used to receiving from the opposite sex. Nor had she tried to engage him in conversation. He would've thought that she was into Omar with the hugs and grins she gave him. But she was doing the same to the next group of young women and men who'd come onboard. Perhaps that was just her personality.

So, why not with him?

Zhi wasn't used to working hard to get a woman's attention. He'd never had to work hard at anything until recently. Perhaps there was a YouTube video on this too?

A quarter hour later and the same indistinct loud music blared as he came back to the main deck. The sound halted him in his tracks. Songs that had no business being together crashed one into the other as though shoving through a door that was too small.

The pulse brought on a headache the closer he got to the source. Unfortunately, he'd have to go right into the eye of the storm because that's where she was.

Parker jumped and swayed and spun at the center of it all. Her multi-colored hair bounced like a rainbow shimmering after a morning's rain. At the end of that rainbow might be a pot of gold. So, with a long sigh, Zhi made his way through the crowd.

He was jostled by bodies jumping not only up and down but side to side. He dodged flailing arms and elbows. No one heard, or simply didn't pay heed, to his calls of excuse me and apologies. Finally, he realized the only way to get through the crowd was to join in on the insanity.

He jumped up and down flailing with the rest of them. No one was more surprised than Zhi when he didn't sustain a single injury in the melee. And then he was right next to her.

For a moment she simply danced alongside him. When Parker finally looked up, surprise lit her dark brown eyes when recognition dawned. She offered his shoulder a squeeze, then she threw her hands up and threw her body even more fervently into the dance.

They continued to dance close. As close as two people could get while jumping and bopping and flailing limbs. It wasn't one of the ballroom dances or partner dances Zhi was accustomed to. He wished he could just pull her close into his arms and gaze into her eyes in order to capture her full attention. Trying to jump in sync wasn't working.

As though the gods of the sea heard him, the beats slowed. Zhi wasn't sure if he was imagining it, but he thought he heard the sounds of a violin mixing in with the drum beats. Was that one of Bach's fugues?

Zhi held still to listen. The notes were unmistakably Bach. Unfortunately, the true mistake was standing still on the dance floor.

The tide had changed. Parker had been swept up. She was now dancing away from him. Before Zhi could make a move to change course, a scratch sounded, and the music changed.

Gone was the soothing keys of Bach. In its place was a Top Twenties chart-topper. The crowd exploded.

Zhi wasn't ready for it. He was bounced around and bumped into and jostled in different directions until he didn't know which way was right or left or up or down. Parker was nowhere to be seen.

He reached out his hand to steady himself and gain his bearings. His hand rested on something that kicked at his fingers. He looked down to see that he was at the massive speakers.

He jerked his head up and took a step back. His back met with a sharp edge. His feet came out from under him. The last thing he heard was the sound of the needle scratching the record of the awful pop song and then blessed silence.

But the silence only lasted a split second as he crashed down and onto the floor.

He put out his hand and tumbled. His fingers wrapped around another pulsing surface. But it was warm and soft and curvy. It was a woman.

Zhi found himself wrapped around a woman with the deepest blue eyes and golden strands of hair. Her lush lips were turned down in a frown. Zhi had the irrational urge to taste that frown. Something in his mind swore that it would be sweet.

The woman's eyes widened as though she saw the trajectory of his thoughts. Her gaze slipped to his lips as well. He would never know if she would give him the go-ahead or shove him off her. The sound of booing jerked their attention back to the crowd of dancers who were all staring down at them.

CHAPTER EIGHT

Spin had just begun her crescendo when the music died, and everything around her came crashing down. She was running over her set time of two hours, but she hadn't felt the slightest bit of fatigue because the crowd was so into it and so responsive.

It was always hard coming into a new club or a new clique, but Spin was a pretty good read of people. The average person could lie with words and tell her they liked a certain type of music. Or that she'd done a good job even when she knew a mix wasn't exactly on the beat. The movement of a crowd of bodies always told the truth.

The small crowd of less than one hundred of Parker's employees and friends had held up the walls when Spin had first dropped the needle. They cast doubtful glances at the disco anthem she began with.

But like the song promised, she soon turned the beat around and the party upside down. When the percussive beat and syncopated rhythms chimed in, the crowd slowly migrated away from the walls and onto the dance floor. The migration continued, and their bodies began to really move as she sped forward in time to the music they knew and loved.

She kept reading them, working them into a frenzy. She dropped an oldie but goodie that was remixed and mashed up with a little acid house beat and the crowd went wild. They were in the palm of her hands.

Until it all came crashing down. Not only had the music stopped, but her body was also tumbling down to the hard ground. She closed her eyes waiting for impact. It never came.

Spin found herself wrapped in warmth and a spicy, expensive hint of musk and ... was that Pine Sol? She was brought back to walking in the woods of Ontario where a deep breath smelled of Christmas and warm fires.

Spin had never had a Christmas tree. She and her mother never stayed in a place long enough to decorate one. But they did spend a lot of time out of doors walking in forests.

The memories assailed her as she was curled inside the man's arms. For the first time in her life, she wanted to stay put and snuggle under a blanket with someone. She wanted to chop down a tree and decorate it with tinsel. She'd been so set to run just a moment ago, but now for the first time in a long time, she wanted to hold still in the silence.

The deafening silence of the party where she was being paid to perform. Spin opened her eyes to find the man staring down at her in concern. His catlike eyes were owl wide as they gazed down at her. Spin found herself lost in their dark depths.

A sparkle of light emanated from around his irises, and she felt warmed through. His gaze dipped to her lips, and she inhaled. Was he about to kiss her? Was she going to let him? Clearly, she was considering it as he was still on top of her, staring down at her, and she hadn't shoved him off.

It was the sound of boos from the crowd that finally brought them both back to their senses.

"I'm so sorry," he said. His voice was honey rich but darker. More like sandalwood which would make sense with the earthy scent coming off his body. "Are you hurt?"

Spin knew she should answer, but she was far too busy picking the tone of his voice apart. She wondered if she could sample its timbre, reproduce it digitally, and play it on a loop. The frequency of it would suit a jazz tempo or a techno beat.

"Are you conscious? Can you open your eyes?" The voice was decidedly European with a bit of a Spanish lilt. But the face peering down at her was decidedly Asian.

Spin felt a calloused finger run along her temple.

She frowned at the texture. It didn't match the smooth, cultured voice. She wasn't complaining. The combo of refinement and roughness felt perfect.

His skin was more honey golden than sandalwood umber. His long nose was proud, and his chin was strong. Spin watched in fascination, her mind recording every note as his lips moved, making more words. He spoke in English. Then switched to French. And finally, he repeated the words in Spanish.

All the while she watched him as though under a trance. She wanted to take the different languages and layer them into the song as well.

He looked up and away from her, concern on his brow. "I think we need a medic."

That's snapped her out of her stupor. She avoided doctors like they were the plague. They asked way too many questions and had access to way too many personal files.

"I'm fine," she managed.

She motioned to sit up as he motioned to peer down at her. In the uncoordinated move, she bumped her for head on his chin. But his lips brushed her temple, and she shuddered.

Aiming to avoid another collision, Spin pressed her hand against his chest intending to push him away. But she felt his heart pounding at her fingertips. The feeling of it reverberated through her entire body. That beat, coupled with his words, played in her head on repeat. She worried that the song of him would get stuck inside her head.

"Spin? Are you okay?"

Spin looked beyond her muse to find Parker making a beeline for them. At the sight of Parker, Spin's savior rose to his full height to greet the woman.

"It's all my fault," he said.

"It was an accident," said Parker, her attention on Spin.

"I'm pretty sure it was my dance moves," he said, with a self-deprecating grin that Spin was certain had demolished many a woman's defenses. "I'm much more adept in a ballroom than on a club dance floor. There it's acceptable to sweep a girl off her feet."

A few of the girls present giggled, their defenses clearly knocked down and busted wide open for him to ransack if he chose. But his gaze was firmly fixed on Parker.

Spin chided herself for thinking that he could've been remotely interested in her. He was clearly there for Parker. He was probably one of her employees aiming to impress her.

Spin rolled to her knees in an effort to regain her footing. But before she could rise, he gave her back a fraction of his attention and put his hand out to her. Not waiting for her to take his hand, he wrapped his big hand around her wrist and hauled her up as though she weighed nothing.

Once again, Spin felt as though warm honey were

running over her skin. That shock of pine scent went straight to her head. But her feelings were apparently only one-sided because as soon as she was on her feet, his attention turned back to Parker.

Spin couldn't help but frown at the total opposites. Parker was dressed to party, while he was dressed for business. Who wore a button down shirt, a tie, and pressed slacks to a rave? And were those dress shoes? He looked like he stepped out of *GQ* while Parker graced the cover of *Wired* magazine. This guy was clearly out of his league.

"Of course, I'll pay for any damages," Parker was saying.

"It was my fault," said Mr. GQ. "I'll cover it."

"It's my party, Your Grace."

Your Grace?

"Please, no need to be so formal," he said. "Just call me Zhi."

"Zhi, I insist I cover the damages. Give me your bank account, Spin d'Elle."

Spin looked between the two. She'd never had people fight over giving her money. Her gaze finally settled on Parker. "I don't have a bank account."

"PayPal account?" Parker asked.

"Nope."

"Bitcoin?"

"I'm a cash-only enterprise." Spin shrugged, unapologetically. "Besides, the set up isn't mine. And there's no need. There's no permanent damage."

Turning back to the tables, she righted the equipment and flipped a few buttons. The music roared back to life. The crowd cheered. Parker fist bumped Spin.

His grace, Zhi, watched the whole exchange with a grimace. Spin had noticed that the grimace had appeared as soon as the music was restarted. But he plastered on a smile when he turned to Parker.

He held out his hand for Parker, like something out of a BBC period movie. Parker looked confused. But she shrugged and took his offering.

Spin turned in the opposite direction, as far away from the graceful Zhi as possible. She knew that honorific was for the titled nobility. She'd be sure to steer clear of him. Nobles were the wrong kinds of people. She didn't appreciate the riffraff coming into her world.

CHAPTER NINE

Sleep eluded Zhi. The party went on into the middle of the night. Music blared until dawn. Just a few hours after sunrise, he finally gave up the pretense of sleep and rose to greet the new day.

All was quiet on deck. The sight was as loud as a riot. The ship had sailed across a calm sea, but the deck looked as though it had been through a war zone.

Bodies littered the chairs and the floor. A few partygoers leaned over the railing paying respect to the sea god with an offering of last night's meal. There were even a few still on their feet, bopping about with earbuds plugged in.

Even at the height of his partying days, Zhi hadn't done it like this. Clubbing had never been his bag. He preferred exclusive clubs with expensive vintages and velvet topped off sections where he and his friends could hear each other's witty remarks. The crowd sat upright. The music was refined. Before turning in for the night, the people had the decency to throw up in their own toilet.

If this was Parker's world, could he see himself in it? He could barely keep his eyes open past two last night. Meanwhile, he'd easily spied her still at the center of the dance floor moving as though she had the energy for another five hours.

The only way he could fathom pursuing her was if they truly had something in common. So far, their music tastes were vastly different. Their sense of style was at polar opposites. They'd barely shared a few sentences let alone a whole conversation.

Maybe this was a mistake. It had to be a mistake. The genesis of the idea had been uttered by his father.

What had Zhi been thinking? He hadn't been thinking. He'd just been desperate for a solution, and this was the lowest hanging fruit.

As soon as the boat docked, he'd have to face reality. He wasn't quite sure what that reality would look like? But he'd stare it down until he had a handle on it or more likely, a wrench.

"You're alive."

Zhi turned to the droll voice. Omar sat perfectly upright at the bar with the stoic posture of his ancestors. He knew the man had likely drunk a few glasses of something, but since his youth, Omar had always been able to hold his drink with no adverse effects. He was also a night owl; he could spring into action on little to no sleep.

"Have you been up all night?" Zhi asked.

Omar shrugged, tipping back an amber liquid. The crystals at the bottom of the mug gave away the fact that the drink was likely tea.

"Most of it," Omar answered. "Been reading scripts and looking over audition tapes for a new show."

"You were able to work with all that racket going on?" Zhi slumped into the seat next to his friend and ordered a black coffee for himself.

"This is your generation." Omar chuckled.

"You're just a few years older than me." Zhi looked at the last ones standing. He couldn't help but notice that the lot of them looked younger than his years. "These people were raised in the wild."

"Snob," Omar snorted.

And maybe he was right. Zhi did like the finer things in life. But he also was partial to modesty when it came to the women he actually wanted to date. A number of girls were walking around in lacy bras that were clearly not waterproofed to be considered as bikini tops. Sure it was a ship's deck, but that was still no cause to walk around barefoot out of doors. Yeah, perhaps he was a snob.

"I like refinement." He had to raise his voice over the pulsing electronic beat that sounded from somewhere in the distance. "I also like real instruments."

"You sound like my mother."

Zhi turned to look over his shoulder. Parker approached. Her riotous colored hair was a divided rainbow in two pigtails. She wore a halter top that was higher than her belly button. He suspected with a stretch of the arms the cropped top would rise immodestly high. The jeans she wore looked as though they were painted on. And her feet ... were bare against the floors.

"My mother hates EDM," she said as she sidled up to the bar.

Zhi struggled with his expression. Should he smile in commiseration? Or should he offer condolences? EDM? Was that a good thing, a bad thing, an actual thing?

"Is that some type of disease?" he asked finally.

Parker's eyebrows rose. It looked like she now struggled with which way to land her expression. The side of her lip tugged in preparation to laugh. But the corner of her eyes narrowed as though preparing to dole out compassion.

"Yeah," said a voice from behind Parker. "My mom wasn't a fan of electronic dance music either."

Last night's DJ enunciated each word from the acronym. Her gaze was on Parker, a grin on her face as she did so. But she slid Zhi a glance, clearly letting him know that she knew that he didn't know what he was talking about.

The moment she slid him her gaze, he latched

onto it. The memory of crashing into her, of holding her body in his arms, of tasting the salty sweetness of her skin muddled his mind. He gave himself a shake, freeing him from her glance, and turned back to Parker. He'd finally found a kernel of a thing they shared in common.

"I have to confess," said Zhi, "I like live music and instrumentals better."

"Yup," said Parker. "Just like my mom."

Zhi held his sigh. So maybe not something directly in common with her. But sharing a passion with her mother, whom he knew she adored, wasn't a bad thing.

"I keep telling her she loved rock 'n' roll," Parker continued. "Which her parents thought was the devil's music."

"My mother loves classical music," said Zhi. "Especially full orchestras. She loves all parts playing both individually and then together as a whole."

Parker nodded thoughtfully, her eyes sliding off into the distance. Zhi's eyes came again to the DJ. Her blue gaze sparkled, as though they delighted at his words. He couldn't be sure, but he thought he heard her whisper *mine too*.

"My mom and I don't see eye to eye on music," said Parker. "But she supports me in my business. She's the best person in the world, and I'd do anything for her."

Parker's dark brown eyes were actually focused on him this time. Zhi felt a warmth spread through his chest. Finally, a true thread between the two of them. The devotion to one's mother was something to build on. But before he could form a sentence, Parker changed the subject.

"Last night was a rage, right?" Her dark eyes were animated. Her brows pulsed up as though she were remembering the loud cacophony from the other night.

Zhi's raging headache from the music threatened to come back. He was certain she didn't share his feelings of annoyance about the noise from the other night. So, what could she possibly mean when she said rage?

Was she using the word as a noun? A verb? Maybe an adverb? But the verb in the sentence was was, wasn't it?

"Yeah," DJ Spin spoke up. "We sure did *party hard* all night. Well, some of us anyway."

Zhi ignored the last bit which she said under her breath and focused on her helpful definition. Oh. Parker had meant the party was a success. Well, maybe not by his standards, but he didn't need to let her know that.

"You didn't look like you were enjoying yourself," said Parker. "You disappeared a little after midnight."

"I ... yeah." Zhi fidgeted. "Well, it wasn't exactly my kind of music. No offense."

That last bit was tossed over to the DJ who was standing with her hands resting on her hips. She shrugged her shoulders. She was also wearing skinny jeans, but her t-shirt was tucked in, and he got no hint of skin. What he did get was a look at the graphic on her t-shirt.

There were two stick figures beneath the five horizontal lines of a music staff. Over top, the head of one stick figure was a rest note. The caption read "Stop. You're under a rest."

When Zhi's gaze traveled back up to DJ Spin's, she simply quirked an eyebrow at him. That eyebrow smirked at him as though to say "Oh, the words on my chest you can comprehend?"

"No offense taken," said Spin. "I'll hook a Stradivarius into the turntables the next time I gig."

"A what?" Now it was Parker's turn to not understand the lingo.

"It's a violin," DJ Spin translated before Zhi could. "It's expensive. Top-of-the-line. But it does make a beautiful sound. I've sampled one before."

"I thought I heard some Bach last night in your ..." Zhi struggled to find the word.

"The word you're looking for is music." Spin's hands moved from her hips to cross over her chest, covering up the rest notation.

There was something about her stance that made him want to go forward, not take a rest, and accept her challenge. He reminded himself that he was in pursuit of someone else. And so he turned back to Parker. "It was a great party."

"Yeah," Parker nodded her agreement. "People got pretty turnt."

Zhi turned back to the DJ, waiting for the translation. She pursed her lips together for a long moment, but finally, she spat it out, spelling it out for him.

"Yeah, things got a little *wild*."

Oh. Turnt meant wild.

"Yeah," said Zhi. "It certainly was turned. Turned me around."

"Well, people are coming down now," said Parker.

"Down to eat breakfast?" said Zhi. "Good, I'm starved."

Parker's raised eyebrow and quizzical expression let Zhi knew he'd misinterpreted again. He looked over to the DJ who rolled her eyes and huffed a sigh.

"I'm sure people will want to eat now that they're coming down from their hangovers."

She spoke in a slow, enunciated fashion as though he were a child. Zhi felt like he was. He swore he'd need a translation guide to keep up with this conversation. But blessedly, Parker ended his misery when she turned to greet her rising employees.

"All right, I'm gonna go check on my people," she said, turning away from Zhi. "Be PLUR."

Zhi looked to the DJ for translation, but Spin only quirked a brow at him and then sauntered off in the opposite direction, leaving him hanging. It didn't matter. No one was left to see his floundering.

"That was extraordinary," said Omar. "I've never seen you bomb before."

Zhi turned back to his friend. He'd completely forgotten the man was there. He hadn't said a word the whole time. Likely because the producer had been far too entertained to stop the show.

"I said come and let your hair down," said Omar. "Not get it tangled up in knots trying to be someone you aren't."

"Was it just me? Or did you only understand about a quarter of that conversation?"

"It's just you." Omar downed the last of his tea. "I live in this world of slang and double entendres. If you want to stay in this magical land for any length of time, maybe you'll want to get yourself a translator."

Omar snorted at the recommendation. He didn't notice that Zhi's look turned thoughtful at the suggestion.

CHAPTER TEN

"You want to do some shopping here before we head back across the sea tonight?"

Lark slung her day bag over her shoulder as they left the room they had shared last night. They had each been given their own room. But Lark had wandered in behind Spin at three in the morning. The two had gabbed all night and then fallen asleep in their clothes.

Spin wheeled her carry-on sized suitcase out the door behind Lark. Everything she cared about was stuffed in its belly. She was the queen of minimalism and the diva of thrifting, which was how her wardrobe always looked so varied and plentiful. Her Bohemian sense of style allowed her to mix and match the essentials and layer on a vintage shirt that only costs a few Euros.

All her music was on a hard drive backed up to the

cloud. She could plug into any turntable anywhere in the world and play. By this time tomorrow, she would be somewhere else in the world, and that place wasn't Nice.

She still hadn't told Lark she wasn't coming back. She would. She wouldn't chicken out and slip away without a word. Even if she and Lark couldn't do any more sleepovers, she still wanted access to sliding into her DM whenever she wanted to. Spin knew she'd only get a response if she didn't disappear into the night like a one-night stand.

Since Spin's mother's death, Lark had been the closest thing to family. Spin hadn't attached herself to many things. As she followed behind a chattering Lark, Spin realized she wasn't quite ready to let her friend go.

A day of shopping wouldn't hurt anything. She was certain that Crepe Man wouldn't be searching for her here on the island nation of Cordoba. It had no connection to her father or his family. Spin's hand went to the necklace resting on her chest.

"Why don't we hang out in Cordoba for the weekend?" she said to Lark. "You don't have a show until next Thursday. I don't have anything lined up for a minute."

"We can't just take an impromptu vacation."

"Why not?"

"We can't afford it for one."

"We can grab a cheap hotel for a few days with the money I just made from Parker."

"And then what?"

Spin shrugged. She'd find a way. She always did.

"Excuse me, Miss ...? I'm sorry, I don't actually know your name."

Spin turned to find his grace himself hurrying up after. She looked left and right and was surprised that Parker was nowhere to be found. The man was clearly into the tech mogul. Though Spin couldn't fathom why. They clearly had nothing in common.

"Can I talk to you for a second in private?" The duke, Zhi he'd called himself, asked.

"You can try," Spin smirked. "But it's clear we don't speak the same language."

"That's what I want to talk to you about," he said.

The cultured accent rolled into her ears. The abundance of T's in his sentence hit a switch, urging her to record the sounds coming from his mouth and place them in the cloud with the rest of her treasures.

He rubbed at the back of his neck as he peered down at her. Spin's gaze traveled to his rolled up sleeve to his tanned bicep. Her throat was suddenly dry. She couldn't remember a man ever making her feel thirsty.

Zhi shrugged his shoulders, the muscles bunching and flexing beneath his shirt. "I know nothing of EMD."

"EDM," she enunciated each letter in the correct order. "Electronic dance music."

He nodded, but his brow was still furrowed showing he clearly didn't understand the topic he was speaking on. Spin bit her lip. She certainly didn't find the expression adorable. Not one bit.

"I don't know much about it or the culture," he said. "But I have an interest in Parker."

Spin's clear gaze darkened. She bit the inside of her lip harder to keep her mouth shut.

"I was hoping you could help me with understanding her?"

"I don't know her," said Spin. "We only just met the other day at a party where she heard me play."

"You two speak the same language. Turned and rages and candy."

The way he spoke the slang, all proper with perfect diction, Spin was sure he spelled them correctly in his mind.

"You also appear to speak my language," Zhi continued. "I'm hoping you can translate. Maybe teach me."

"Teach you what? To be a rave bunny?"

The hand that had been at his neck now rose to scratch at his temple. "I don't even know what that means?"

Spin glanced over to the side at Lark. Her friend was listening intently to the conversation. She was also eying the candy shaped man in front of them. Spin turned back to him as well. There was sugar in her voice as she spoke to clarify his distasteful suggestion.

"Okay. I'll put it in your language. You want me to be your Cyrano de Bergerac so that you can seduce Parker?"

His dark gaze lit with understanding. "Yes."

"No." Spin spat the word out in disgust.

He was taken aback. Literally. His shoulders straightened, and his chest puffed up. Spin had to look away from the display.

"Why not?" he asked.

"Because I don't help men trick women."

"It's not a trick. It's a translation."

Spin still frowned her disgust up at him.

"I'll pay you."

"Oh." The word came out as a long sigh. She took a deep breath as her disgust turned to anger. "Well, in that case; definitely not. I'm not gonna pimp my skills and be your prose prostitute."

"Sorry." He held up his hands in a stop motion. "That's not my intention at all."

Sure it was. He was a duke, nobility. Men like him thought they could have any woman they wanted and then drop them. She knew exactly what his intentions were. She knew exactly the type of man he was. But she wasn't used to hearing a man like him say sorry for any reason.

"I'm used to people wanting money," Zhi said. "Or favors from me. I'm not used to asking for help or handouts. I've botched it, haven't I?"

"Yeah. You did."

But her words were cautious. She wasn't sure of the trajectory of this conversation. He sounded like he was truly sorry. At the same time, he admitted to why she knew he was wrong. She was entirely confused.

"Why would you even want to be with someone like her?" Spin asked.

"It seems we have a lot in common—aside from our tastes in music."

Spin didn't see that they had anything in common. Except maybe their wealth. "Is it because she's rich like you?"

He grimaced. Spin knew it was the height of ill-breeding to discuss money out in the open. But what could she say? Her beginnings were low.

"You know, there's probably an eHarmony for rich people to help them find each other."

He shoved his hands in his pockets. "There probably is. But I've already met her. I just wanted to see if she might be a match already here in real life."

"You could probably get any girl you want as a duke."

"What if I weren't? Would a woman still be interested in me without my title or my money? If you strip away those things that I was born with and look at what's left, what then?"

His words hit her. He stood there before her vulnerable and bare. It was only words; she knew it wasn't reality. But she couldn't take her eyes off him after he'd peeled back those outer layers and gave her a glimpse into his soul.

"Come on, Spin." Lark finally broke her silence. "Help a duke out. You can teach him a couple of things over lunch."

"Where are you staying?" he asked.

"We hadn't figured that out yet." Spin began as she looked to Lark who hadn't agreed to the overnight trip.

"You can stay with me," said Zhi. "I have a large estate. Plenty of room for you and your friend."

CHAPTER ELEVEN

"He's never brought anyone home." Lin's voice came through loud and clear over the phone even though she wasn't the one holding the device.

"I didn't know he was dating." That voice was clearly Allana's who sounded as though she were standing just behind her sister.

"Is she pretty?" That distant shout came from Mathis, though Zhi would've bet the teenager was attempting to whisper the question to those gathered around the phone. "I bet she's a model."

"He said she's not a date." That last voice was Oswald's. His voice was crisp and clear as he was the one holding the phone to his ear.

Zhi pinched the bridge of his nose as he waited for the fever on the other end of the line to die down. He knew better than to try and talk over his staff when they were firing questions one after the other. They couldn't hear him since he was only in Oswald's ear. The butler's attention was diverted to the three people around him, and he wouldn't be listening to Zhi with the cacophony in his other ear.

"She's not a date," Zhi said patiently once he had Oswald's attention once more. "She's going to be working for me."

"Begging your pardon, Your Grace," said Oswald. "But can we afford that?"

To someone else, it might have been an impertinent question. But to Zhi, it showed respect. He was the one in debt. Oswald, Lin, Allana, and Mathis could all leave that morning if they chose. Instead, they chose to stick by him and his family.

Well, maybe not his entire family. But the staff swore they'd never leave the duchess and young duke as long as they breathed. So, they were all a *we*. It wasn't just Zhi's life and his livelihood. If he failed at this, they were all out of luck and out of a home.

After getting Spin's agreement, Zhi had resolved himself to the course of action. He would find common ground with Parker Paley-Li. He would build a bridge to her heart, and he would treasure her for the rest of her days. With DJ Spin's help, of course.

Looking up, Zhi saw that the object of his intentions was seeing her guests and employees off as they disembarked from the ship and onto Cordovian soil. Her rainbow hair swished and shimmered as she threw back her head and laughed. She reached out for hugs and turned here and there.

Zhi could definitely see himself with such a sunny and positive person. She was also clearly brilliant in light of the business she'd built. And everyone around her, especially her employees, all adored her. Just another thing they had in common.

Spin and her friend, Lark, were next in line to say their farewells. Zhi's gaze rested on the young DJ. She was smiling up as her friend chattered on. There was something guarded in that smile. Like the door to her heart was open, but the windows were closed.

"She doesn't require a cash payment," Zhi said into the phone as he moved closer to the group of women at the edge of the ship. "Only food and lodging. So, we'll need to make up a room on the second floor."

There was a moment's silence as that edict translated. They rarely, more like never, had visitors. Precisely because of what lurked on the third floor. Zhi would have to pray his father stayed lucid and quiet during Spin's brief stay. He didn't want his father to slip up and tell his guests the genesis of his interest in dating Parker.

"I'll be home in about an hour or so."

"We'll take care of it, sir," said Oswald, his voice somber and heavy with the new responsibilities put on all of them.

By the time Zhi hung up, he'd reached Parker,

Spin, and Lark. Lark was being enveloped in a tight hug by Parker.

"I'm so glad you two made it," Parker was saying. "Next time I'm in Nice, I'm definitely stopping by your show."

"Oh, please don't," Lark insisted. "You'll be bored to tears."

"More likely, she'll laugh at the bumbling magician as he tries to pull a rabbit out of his hat," said Spin.

The two friends giggled as though they'd shared a private joke. Spin turned to Parker. The two women executed a complicated handshake before embracing.

"Hey there, Your Grace," said Parker after she released Spin.

Zhi knew his fair share of handshakes. He was sure he could repeat the two women's maneuverings if he concentrated. He held out his fist, but Parker laughed and brushed it away. She reached open her arms for a hug.

"It was so awesome to meet you, Zhi," Parker said as she squeezed tight.

She smelled of something sugary sweet and tartly herbal. It wrinkled Zhi's nose, and he held his breath so he didn't sneeze in her hair. She was mostly skin and bones, but there were a few womanly curves beneath her sparse layers of clothing.

"We should get together while you're in my lands," he said when they pulled apart. "I can show you around the nightlife if you'd like."

"That would be awesome. I'd love to see your crib."

Zhi held onto his tight smile while he slid his gaze over to DJ Spin. He worried for a second that she wouldn't help him out. But she rolled her eyes and sighed out a bored response.

"Yeah," Spin said. "I'll bet his grace's *house* is pretty awesome."

"My house?" parroted Zhi. Crib meant house? Was Parker asking to be invited over? "Yes, I'd love to have you over. There are parts that are currently under renovations, though. It's an old house. Maybe we can do dinner instead?"

"That'd be dope," Parker said. "Shoot me a DM on Insta or hit me up on Snap."

Spin opened her mouth to translate, but Zhi wasn't that out of touch. He had both Instagram and Snapchat on his cell.

"I'll do that," he said. "Or I could just get your number."

Spin cringed. Lark chewed at her lower lip and turned away.

"My phone number?" Parker cocked her head to the side and frowned. "What for?"

"Well ... I ..." Zhi looked to Spin, but she was shaking her head. He knew she wanted him to shut his mouth, but he had no clue where he'd just gone wrong? Why use the texting features of social media when they could just talk directly over the phone?

As though she saw the trajectory of his thoughts,

Spin looped her arm through his and steered him toward the gangway. "We should probably get going, Your Grace."

"Oh." Parker's brows rose with interest. "Are you two together?"

"No," Zhi said hastily. "I'm just giving Spin and Lark a ride into town."

"Oh, cool." Parker turned to Spin. "You're staying. We definitely need to hang out again, DJ Spin d'Elle."

"Bet," said Spin. "Be easy, Parker."

"Be PLUR, Parker," said Zhi. And then he felt a yank on his arm.

"Stop talking," Spin growled under her breath.

"What did I say wrong? I read up on PLUR. Peace Love Unity and Respect. Did I use it wrong?"

"How old are you?" Spin said gazing up at in with incredulity. "It's like you're from another century."

CHAPTER TWELVE

The duke's manspread invaded Spin's space inside the confines of the luxury car. Spin turned her body away from him and toward the window, gazing out at her first sights of Cordoba. From the opposite side of the luxury car, Lark and Omar, another nobleman of the country, filled the silence. It would appear that the Marquis of Navarre was also in the entertainment industry.

Beside her, the Duke of Mondego stared at his phone. Spin's gaze fixed on how he caressed the slim device in the palm of his large hands. His thumb carefully slid back and forth over the face. A bump in the road loosed the phone from his grip, and it spilled into Spin's lap.

She reached down and picked it up preparing to hand the phone back to him. She stopped in her tracks when she saw Parker's smiling photo grinning back at her. It was her Instagram profile.

Spin's gaze cut to Zhi's. "Were you about to DM her just now?"

"Yes." His hand was outstretched, patiently waiting to take his property back. "What's wrong with that?"

He made a motion for his phone. When she still gripped it tightly in her palm, he reached over and tried to take his phone back. Spin yanked it from him and toward the window so that he'd have to cross her body in order to retrieve it. Finally, he gave up and raised his brows at her with a questioning glance that told her he had no clue as to the colossal mistake he almost made.

"You just left her," Spin accused.

His brows quirked, one up, one down in that adorable way he'd done earlier. "I thought girls liked guys being direct, going after what they wanted, and not taking days to do it."

Spin wouldn't know? She'd never had a guy show that kind of interest in her.

"As your translator," she said, "you're not going to message her five minutes after leaving her presence. That translates to desperate and creepy."

Zhi sighed, the sound impatient. His knees bumped hers as he turned to face her. "She's not here for long. I don't want to miss my opportunity. When can I contact her?"

"Give it at least twelve hours."

"So, dinner time?" He looked at his watch. He tapped a few dials.

Spin could see that he was setting a reminder. She shook her head and turned to his friend, the marquis. "Is he always like this?"

"I don't know?" Omar's gaze was filled with amusement. "I've never actually seen him chase after a girl. They usually fall into his lap, sometimes while he's still standing up."

"I'm not chasing," Zhi protested.

The other three sets of eyes in the car looked at him as though they begged to differ.

"I find her interesting," Zhi said.

"I think it's romantic," said Lark. "It could be love at first sight."

Spin snorted. Parker was very attractive. And Zhi, well, he had his charms. He may have been staring at Parker, but she'd hardly given him a second glance. Was that the game? Was Zhi only interested in Parker because she didn't fall immediately into his lap?

"What do you like about Parker?" Lark pressed.

Zhi thought for a minute. A full minute. And then for a couple of seconds more. "She's intelligent. A self-starter. She clearly has a great head for business."

"Sounds great," said Omar. "If you were interviewing her for a job."

Spin agreed. Something was off about this whole affair. But she couldn't put a finger on it.

Initially, after meeting Omar, she had wondered if

it were a bet between these two noblemen. The whole can the hot guy seduce the nerdy girl plot. But Omar was just as perplexed about the attraction as she was.

"When I get to know her a little bit better, then I'll know more." Zhi shrugged. "Isn't that what dating is all about?"

No one answered. Spin got the inkling that it might have been because none of the others in the car had truly dated. She knew that she and Lark had never had a serious relationship. Omar didn't look the type to wine and dine a woman. He looked like the kind of man who would conquer a woman and then leave her begging for more as he moved on. Swarthy, that was the best word to describe the dark man.

When the marquis caught her staring at him, he winked. Spin narrowed her gaze. She could tell he meant nothing by it. It was probably a reflex when he saw someone of the female persuasion.

The car slowed as they crossed a bridge over sparkling blue waters. From the canopy of lush trees, the house rose. It was as though the car transformed into a carpet, and they were sailing toward an enchanted castle.

"Welcome to Mondego House," said the duke. There was clear pride in his voice. A touch of awe as well as he surveyed his homestead.

House was a misnomer. A house was something at the end of a cul de sac. This was across a mote. There were at least three stories, maybe four. Just the spires alone were their own entity. The sun cast the face of the house in a golden hue, and the rays shimmered on each of the many windows.

The car came to a stop before stone steps. A tall man dressed in a dark suit stood at the end of the steps. He came forward and opened the door. He bowed, offering his hand to Spin.

Spin hesitated. Though she had a healthy distaste for the upper class, especially those of blue blood, her mother had raised her with manners. Spin placed her fingers lightly in the man's hand and was met with calluses.

Though he may be a front of the house servant, he clearly got his hands dirty. She gripped him more tightly, allowing him to alight her from the car.

"Greetings, my lady," he said.

Spin took her hand away. "I'm not a lady."

He simply smiled. "My apologies, Miss ...?"

Spin stepped to the side as Zhi came out behind her, followed by Lark. Omar gave a salute before shutting the door. The car pulled off and headed back over the bridge.

"Welcome home, Your Grace," said the man, bowing in deference to his employer. "I trust your trip went well?"

"It did indeed," said Zhi. "We have guests. This is Lark Voorhees and ..." Zhi turned to Spin, eyeing her curiously. "You know, I don't know your real name."

"Neither do I," said Lark. "I've known her over a

year, and she's only ever gone by Spin d'Elle. Don't bother trying to get it out of her. She's a master at evasive techniques. I tell her she should've been a magician, but I secretly think she's in the Witness Protection Program."

Spin ignored them and instead climbed the steps, neatly evading the topic of conversation. The front door was thrown open by a woman dressed in a black and white maid's uniform. She smiled with interest at Spin.

Inside, the house was grand. Something out of a dusty fairytale book. Old but not exactly out of date. The furniture looked as though it had been around since before the Victorian age. It was well kept, but signs of wear and tear were visible if you knew where to look, which Spin did.

"May I help you with your luggage, miss?" said the maid who'd opened the door.

"I got it," said Spin. "You don't have to wait on me."

The woman smiled jovially. Her hair was in a perfect bun making Spin wonder just how good she was at cleaning all day if she didn't have a hair out of place. "It's my job and my pleasure. Miss ..."

"DJ Spin d'Elle. Or you can just call me Spin."

"Oh, how clever," said the maid. "Spindle like the spinning wheel needle."

Coming up from behind her, Zhi let out a laugh. "I didn't get that. It is clever."

Why did his praise warm her? Why did his smiles send tingles down her spine?

He walked up to Spin. Swaggered was more like it. She felt like a doe caught in the sight of a lean and hungry tiger. He held out his hand to her. Spin's instinct was to clasp her hand with his and not let go.

"I'll take my property back now," he said.

Cold dread wash over her. Her hand immediately went to the jewel at her neck. "I didn't take anything."

He grinned, showing his incisors. "Yes, my lady, you did."

Spin gulped. Instinct warned her to take a step back, to run. But her body was immobile, trapped under his gaze.

"My phone," Zhi said.

She swallowed and then had to swallow again before she could speak. "Don't call me a lady." She slapped his phone into the palm of his outstretched hand. "And don't go on social media without my permission."

He let out a low laugh. A sound that Spin was sure a hungry tiger toying with his food would make. Then he bowed and turned on his heel. His steps were regal as he walked through his domain.

CHAPTER THIRTEEN

Zhi ran his thumb over his phone. Parker's Instagram profile smiled back at him. It was the longest he'd held her gaze since they'd met. Typically, by this time with any other interaction, a woman was already sliding into his various social media inboxes. But all his alerts were silent.

He had the urge to press his pursuit by tapping the little paper airplane icon in the corner of the app. But Spin's glare and waggling finger arrested his actions. He'd never thought about waiting to contact a woman for a prescribed period. He also had never chased after a woman. Or slid into her DM for that matter. He was usually the one responding, not launching the airplane icon.

Women had always been available to him. He honestly had expected to be bringing Parker home to meet his mom today rather than a DJ to tutor him on how to communicate with the woman he was interested in.

Zhi depressed his thumb, swiping off Parker's profile. He tapped the magnifying glass icon and did a search for his new house guest. Because he didn't know her real name, he typed in her stage moniker.

He tried DJ Spin but got a large number of results. Placing the cursor at the end, he added d'Elle. No picture of a woman popped up, but he knew he had found her.

There was a picture of a turntable and her hands. He wasn't sure how he knew, but he knew those were her hands. They'd been on his skin briefly, but they'd left an imprint. Enough for his mind to identify the slender digits in a grainy photograph.

Zhi tore his gaze away from her hands and glanced at the information of her profile. There were hardly any details about her. In fact, there were none. No birth date. No hometown. No school. No relationship. It was like she was a digital ghost.

And yet he was allowing this woman to dictate the course of his life. His thumb traveled back to the top of the phone screen. He gave the paper airplane icon a decisive tap.

Are you in the DJ witness protection program?

A few seconds later her reply came back. *That's something a creepy stalker would ask.*

Zhi chuckled and put his phone away. She could

keep her secrets. Goodness knew he had his own under lock and key.

He knocked lightly on his mother's door. After her gentle acknowledgment, he let himself in. She was sitting in her favorite chair; a royal blue wingback with gold trim. He could tell he'd woken her from the glazed look in her eyes.

"You're back."

"I am," he said. "I think I found a solution."

Her petite form straightened in the chair, but she was still small inside its large cushioned wings. "Another bank?"

Zhi hesitated to go into details. He wasn't trying to trick Parker. He was truly trying to find a common ground that they might build a future on. If it turned out that ground was just a few rocky pebbles, then he'd ... he wasn't sure what he'd do.

"I've made some new friends," he settled on. "I think one might be able to help. In fact, I brought a couple of new friends home to help me ... figure some things out."

"We have guests?" She sat up even taller. "You haven't brought any of your guy friends over in a long while."

"They're not guys. They're two women."

Now her brows rose. Zhi had never brought a female home, friend or more.

"It's not like that *mǔqīn*. It's ... they're helping me

with something. Anyway, you get back to your rest while the beast is at bay."

"Don't call him that," his mother snapped. She came to her feet, all four foot eight of her.

Zhi backed down. His mother might be small, but she was a lioness when it came to those she loved. Regardless of whether they deserved it or not.

"He is your father," she said, her quiet voice a low roar that brooked no argument unless he wanted his head bit off. "He's kept a roof over your head, clothes on your back, and food in your belly all these years."

Zhi couldn't help it. The only way he'd swallow that falsity was if his head were removed from his body. "He is the reason all that may be taken away now."

"You will still respect him." His mother's soft voice was firm. Her dark eyes were hard as flint.

Zhi was too tired to argue. He let his head bow, and then he took his mother's outstretched hand. He helped her climb onto her massive bed that she'd always slept in alone. His father's former chambers adjoined this room as he preferred to keep separate quarters. Zhi pulled the covers up and around his mother and kissed her forehead. With that duty done, he left the room.

A warm shower, a change of clothes, and a glass of wine later, he felt almost like himself. Oswald entered his rooms and showed him the new list of things that needed his attention. Staring at the list, Zhi wished his father was in charge of the mess he'd made, and he could simply be a kid again. But that ship had sailed.

Zhi rolled up his sleeves and got to work, making certain to steer clear of the second floor where his guests were resting. It was midday when Zhi sat the list aside and snuck into the music room.

The room was sparsely decorated. Just white walls, shelves upon shelves of records, CDs, and sheet music. At the center of the large room was a grand piano.

Zhi walked over to it as though it was an oasis, and he was moving across a desert. Playing had always been an escape for him. For his mother as well. They'd both always wound up here after one of his father's rages. The man never came into the room. It was as though he were the Wicked Witch of the West, and he wouldn't breach the barrier of their oasis.

Zhi ran his fingers over the keys. He didn't plan what he'd play. He never did. He simply let his fingers lead. He wasn't surprised that the melody that came from him was the fugue he'd heard the other night aboard the cruise ship.

Only this time, there was no pulsing beat beneath it. Just the sound of the sharps and flats of the grand instrument. There had always been something about the repetition of the notes that calmed him. When the song circled back around and ended as it began, Zhi felt a sense of serenity wash over him, much like after his mother played in the aftermath of one of his father's violent storms.

The silence as the last note died was a comfort. But he knew that he wasn't alone. Knowing his mother was sound asleep, and that none of the staff ever intruded when either he or his mother played, Zhi knew it had to be one of his guests.

He looked up to find DJ Spin leaning against the door jamb. Her cell phone was held up in her hand, aimed at him. But he didn't see a button to indicate that the video record function was engaged.

"What are you doing?" he asked.

"Sampling you," she said as she walked in the room.

"Don't you need my permission?"

"No one own sounds." She smirked, never taking her eyes off her phone as she took a spot on the bench next to him.

"Music is copyrighted."

Now she glanced up at him. "Did you get Bach's permission to play that song?"

Zhi leaned his elbow on top of the piano and turned his body to face her. "For someone who plays underground clubs, you certainly have a grasp of chamber music."

"It's music." She shrugged. "It's all music. I don't believe in labeling sounds."

"Not even polka?" Zhi's shoulders shuddered even as he spoke the offensive word.

"What have you got against polka?"

Instead of waiting for his response, she pushed a

button on her phone. Before he could stop her, the heavy, high-winded beats began.

Zhi groaned like a child being told to eat his vegetables. He would prefer the most cruciferous of veggies to the torment of the Polish pandemonium. But then Spin's hands went to the keys of the piano.

Her fingers glided over the blacks and whites perfectly executing the fugue he'd just finished. Somehow, she timed it to the beat of the polka. He watched her, enthralled, amazed, disbelieving what he was hearing. Until she stopped abruptly.

Zhi wanted to protest. Before he could, she turned to him and clapped her hands. She clapped once. And then twice more in half the time. She repeated the one-one-two clapping in succession. All while gazing expectantly at him.

It took him a second to realize she wanted him to clap his own hands to the beat. He did so, adding another layer of sound. Once he did, she returned to her playing.

Somehow, the three different strands of music blended into ... something new. She was truly a translation genius if she could take polka, classical, and hand clapping and play them all together into harmony. He felt pulled in by the music notes swirling around them, pulling them into a melody all their own.

Her eyes shut as she played. A grin tugged at the corner of her lips. She looked like she was in heaven.

She looked like an angel. She opened her eyes to catch him staring.

Suddenly, Zhi felt thirsty and hungry at the same time. When was the last time something sweet had passed his mouth? When was the last time he'd had his belly filled with a satisfying morsel?

His errant thoughts caused him to miss the beat. Her finger skipped a key, hitting the wrong note. They both jerked their hands down to their sides at the same time. There was an awkward moment of silence that stretched a second too long.

Finally, Spin rose. "Sounds like you need to get this thing tuned."

"Yeah," he said.

She nodded. Then without another word, she turned on her heel and headed out the room.

Zhi glanced down at the keys. He'd never played for anyone other than his mother. But he'd just made music with Spin. It felt exhilarating. But it also left him feeling a little exposed.

He reached down and pulled the keyboard cover shut. He would need to tune the instrument. Just another thing to add to his ever growing to do list.

CHAPTER FOURTEEN

Spin slumped down on the bed. A plume of dust came up from the pillows. She frowned down at the small particles making a mess of the noble air.

She had taken a nap after being shown to the room she would spend the night in. Lark was next door, likely still fast asleep. But Spin had been a light sleeper all her life, and so she'd been up and about in just an hour.

The sound of music had lulled her to the music room. She hadn't been entirely surprised to find the lord of the manor seated at the grand piano. She had been surprised at the wrong note she struck on the magnificent instrument.

Surely, they'd have had it tuned on a regular basis. The keys had sounded off as Zhi had been playing, but the passion he'd put into the simple song had been so compelling. The piano was likely well-loved and well used.

His playing had been so haunting. So layered. She wanted to pull back the man's layers, stanza by stanza, to get to the heart of him.

Spin shook herself of the ridiculous notion. She wasn't pulling anything off the Duke of Mondego. She wasn't getting underneath anything.

The guy was interested in the heart of another woman. Spin wasn't trying to give her heart to anyone. Especially someone of the noble class. They were all scoundrels and liars, the lot of them.

Worse yet, she still had the nagging feeling the Zhi was hiding something. She didn't care to find out what. She'd take advantage of his food and lodging while she planned her next move.

A creak overhead forced her to sit upright. She stared at the ceiling, uncertain if what she'd just heard was an animal moaning as though it were in pain? Or just the bones of an old house settling its weight.

The wail sounded again. That was not the sound of joints and floorboards digging into the earth. That was the sound of something very much alive clinging to life.

Spin put her feet on the floor and heard the creek again. She paused. Uncertainty racing down her spine.

Maybe that had come from her weight on the floorboards? But she was a connoisseur of sound. She felt certain it had come from above. Maybe someone was walking above on the forbidden third floor?

But there was another sound. This time in the walls. It sounded to her like the twisting of metal, perhaps a faulty pipe?

She listened intently but didn't hear the life-like groan again. Just the clanging of pipes and the creaking of floorboards. It was probably just all in her head, like the thought that the duke was about to lean down and kiss her back in the music room.

Spin shook herself, trying to divest her wild imagination from that thought. As her body shuddered with the heat of that irrational impossibility, she shifted her weight from foot to foot. The creaking sound was definitely coming from her added weight on the floor. The sounds of monsters in the walls, the thoughts of royal kisses, they were all in her head.

Still, it was strange. She would never in her wildest dreams go for a guy like Zhi Mondego. He was a duke. Spin hated the noble class, especially after what they did to her family.

She'd gotten her revenge, though. And she'd never give them a chance to take it from her. The only way that beast would ever get his hands on her was over her cold dead body.

Unfortunately for her, the blue bloods had long memories and deep pockets. She knew they would never stop looking for her to retrieve what they thought was theirs. Spin pressed the necklace to her heart.

Another low moan sounded from overhead. It was not the floorboards. It was not the pipes. It was not her belly. There was something, or someone, up there.

She reached for the door. Yanking it open she let out a high pitched squeal. "You scared me."

Lark stood there. Hand raised as though poised to knock. She lowered her hand and regarded Spin with concern. "What's wrong? You look like you've seen a ghost."

"I just ..." Spin looked up, then down, then at the walls. All was silent in the hall. "I just thought I heard something."

"Old house," said one of the maids.

She was standing just behind Lark. She gave Spin a curtsey which had Spin grimacing. Spin was staunch in her beliefs that no human should ever bow to another. But she held her tongue as the pretty young maid introduced herself as Allana, the sister to Lin.

"There are lots of noises in this old house," Allana said. "I don't think I could sleep in silence after living here."

The woman smiled, but it didn't reach her eyes. Yup, there was definitely something out of the ordinary going on here in House Mondego. But Spin decided she didn't want to know what. She was only here for one day, and then she'd be gone. The house and its occupants could keep their secrets. Goodness knew she had enough of her own to worry about.

"There are repairs going on above," Allana continued. "That's why it's best to stay to this floor."

"I got lost," said Lark. "Allana and Mathis here found me."

Spin hadn't noticed the young boy lurking at the corner of the hall. He came forward. It was easy to tell the boy was the offspring of the butler. They had the same dark hair and eyes.

"I find that funny," said Mathis. "A magician getting lost. Can't you just magic yourself where you want to be?"

"I'm a magician's assistant," Lark corrected.

"She does all the work." Spin corrected her friend. "The magician waves his hands, but his assistant is truly the one behind all the tricks."

"Isn't that always the way of it," muttered Allana. "I'd love to see a show where it was all turned around. You know, where the magician bumbles about, but you can see the assistant is the one with the real magic."

Lark's gaze perked up at that. She was unusually silent, lost in thought as the foursome walked down the great hall. Spin hoped she was seriously considering the idea. Lark deserved her own show, especially one where it was clear that she was the brains of the operation.

Spin's attention was diverted to the historical and cultural lesson on display. On the walls hung portraits of the Mondego lineage. She saw many a golden Spaniard with dark hair and curled mustaches. They were often standing or seated next to pale women of certain European descent. That was until the last portrait of a looming man with mischief in his eyes standing beside a small Asian woman.

The woman was the David to his Goliath, but there was a quiet strength about her. Unlike the other portraits where both the woman and the man looked straight ahead, her gaze was on her husband. The woman's eyes were bright, love flowed from the picture as she gazed at the man.

"That is the previous Duke and Duchess," said Allana.

"They've passed away?" asked Spin.

"No." There was something in the maid's voice that Spin couldn't pinpoint. "The duchess is well and in residence. She doesn't prefer to receive visitors. His grace is very ill, which is why his son has taken over his duties. The old duke is not much longer for this world."

Spin noted that Allana didn't sound remorseful at the thought of her former employer's demise. They walked on and came to the portrait of the current Duke of Mondego. There was the light of joy in Zhi's eyes that Spin had seen in his mother's loving gaze. There was also the shadow of mischief that she'd seen in his father's calculating gaze.

"The current Duke Mondego is the best kind of

people," said Allana. Pride was clear in her voice now. "He has his mother's talent. He can play the piano as though it were crafted just for him. We all thought he would become a professional musician. But he only ever plays for his mother in the music room. He's never played in public."

He had just played for her. Well, Spin had barged in. But she'd had the sense that he knew she was there. And he hadn't made her feel that she'd imposed afterward.

"His grace is a dutiful man," Allana continued. "He took over the estate when ... When his father's health declined. I don't know where we would all be without the man."

It was unlike the noble men Spin new from her past. They were all selfish and cared nothing of those they considered beneath them. Zhi was a walking contradiction. But she'd had enough of nobility and being beneath their notice for a lifetime. She had no intention of unraveling the mystery of Zhi Mondego.

CHAPTER FIFTEEN

*L*ater that afternoon, just before dinner, Zhi sat behind his formal desk. It was nearing the prescribed time when he'd be allowed to contact Parker.

He'd changed out of his casual travel clothes and into something more formal. It felt like armor. He needed the added layer of protection after this afternoon and his run-in with the DJ. Spin had a way of getting under his skin, seeing things about him he had no intention of sharing.

He didn't usually play for anyone but his mother. It was something that was personal between the two of them. Music was private, like prayer. It should be done in one's home and not out in the open for the masses to see and pick apart.

But he hadn't felt that way with Spin. He'd felt open. He'd wanted to share. He'd wanted to play with her, like a kid with a new toy. The new sound they'd created together had delighted him. So much so that he could've kissed her.

Of course, he hadn't. It had just been appreciation. That was all.

Though he couldn't deny there was something attractive about her heart-shaped face. Her lips were the same bow shape. Her top lip dipped in like the M shape of a heart's top half. Her bottom lip was plump and lush. Perfect for sinking teeth into.

"You wanted to see me?"

Zhi looked up and scowled at the woman in the doorway. Spin had snuck into his thoughts when he was supposed to be thinking about another woman. She'd also snuck up on him again.

She wore a simple pair of cotton cargo pants and a bandana around her blonde hair. Looking at her, Zhi found himself swallowing a few times. He'd seen women dressed in ball gowns and in their birthday suits. Such a simply clad body should have no effect on him. He crossed his legs beneath the table and scowled deeper.

Ignoring his ducal look of displeasure, she rolled her eyes and slipped inside the office. Coming into the room, she dipped a curtsy that reeked of mockery. "You wanted to see me, *Your Grace*?"

He nearly told her to leave the ceremony but didn't. He found the formality a necessary barrier between them. She was there to do a job. This was a transaction. He'd use her skills, her knowledge, to advance his cause. His cause was to gain the attention of Parker who could help him in saving his home and the people he loved.

"Have a seat Miss ..."

He was annoyed he didn't have that added barrier of formality between them. He still didn't know her real name. He had no clue who this woman truly was. She guarded the details of her life like an encrypted file.

What was she hiding? What might she take from him if he took his eyes off her? She could be a criminal.

Spin eyed him with a taunting smile, as though she knew the trajectory of his thoughts. Her lifted brow dared him to ask.

He didn't. There wasn't much of value left in the estate. His father had sold off every heirloom worth more than a red cent to pay his debts. All that was left was fake or of sentimental value.

Besides, Spin would be leaving shortly. After she helped him out with this last task.

"I've waited the agreed upon hours before contacting Parker," he said. "It's time."

"That's a good boy," Spin mocked.

Zhi grit his teeth. His tone was pleasant and professional when he spoke. "Please, help me craft this text message to her. Then you can help me with a bit of lingo while we wait for the response."

Spin held her hand out for his phone. "Let's see what you got, lover boy."

Instead of his phone, he offered her a sheet of legal paper.

He watched her eyes rapidly read over what he'd composed. "This is a letter."

"Yes." Zhi nodded.

Spin shook her head. She leaned over his desk and snatched his phone before he could react. By the time he made it around the desk and the barriers he'd erected, she was hitting send.

He looked down at the missive that would start his pursuit. It read; *sup*.

No upper case letters or punctuation in sight. Just those three simple letters that made no sense.

"Sup? What does that even mean?"

"What is up?" She enunciated every word.

"In what language?"

Spin ignored him. Three dots inside a bubble appeared on his phone's face. Then disappeared. Then appeared again.

"Should I clarify?" said Zhi. "Should we type all three of those words followed by a question mark?"

Spin yanked the phone out of his reach and frowned at him, exasperation clear on her pretty face. A ding sounded, alerting them that there was a response. Spin pulled the phone back to her so that they both could read.

It read: *chillaxing*.

Still no upper case letters. No punctuation.

"Is that even English?" he asked.

Spin sighed and pursed her lips.

"What?" Zhi bent over her looking from the two-worded conversation and back to her scrunched face. "What's wrong?"

"It's a declarative statement," she said.

"What's that mean?" he said. He knew what a declarative statement was. But not in that context.

"She didn't elaborate."

"That's bad?"

"It means she's not thinking about you."

Zhi straightened. That was bad.

"Don't worry, Romeo. I've got this."

Spin started typing again. He was gratified to see that it was more than a three letter word. And there was a capitalized letter. Though still no punctuation.

My head still ringing from all that base spin dropped

"Why are you making this about you?" Zhi asked.

"I'm your common link," Spin said. "We need to get her chatting."

The bubble burst immediately this time with a message. *That chicks got wicked skillz.*

Spin typed: *True dat. That song by Gkat was boss. I had to nap after that.*

Gkat is dope. U heard his new song?

Spin tapped out three fire emojis followed by: *Yass, it gave me life.*

"Wait?" said Zhi, trying to keep up with the foreign

words and mostly failing. But he did recognize some. "I know that guy, Gkat. He's playing at Omar's club."

Spin took that tidbit and typed; *you rolling up on them at omers tmrw?*

"His name is spelled with an A—"

"Shh!" Spin admonished him.

Parker typed; *sure nuff.*

Spin typed; *c u there.*

A peace sign emoji was Parker's response. And then the bubble went silent.

Spin handed Zhi back his phone.

"Wait?" he said. "That's it?"

She nodded.

"So, we have a date?"

"Not a date," said Spin. "A hangout. People our age don't one-on-one date. We hang out in groups."

Zhi glared down at his phone. "I wanted to spend time alone with her, to get to know her."

"Well to do that you'll have to entice her from the pack."

"How do I do that?"

"Charm her pants off."

"Be serious," Zhi huffed.

"I am. This is the new world. Unless you're going for the straight hook up, you need to hang with the friends and get in with everybody first."

"She's only here for a few days. I don't have time for that."

"What's the rush?" Spin leaned back in the chair. She crossed her arms over her chest and regarded him.

She was wearing a new t-shirt today. This one read Weapons of Mass Percussion. The corner of Zhi's mouth quirked up a bit before he remembered her question.

He opened his mouth and closed it. Those eyes saw right through him. He felt the urge to tell Spin the truth. But the shame in his chest stopped him.

He told the emotion to get lost. He wasn't doing anything shameful. He was trying to get to know a woman to see if they were compatible. And if it turned out they were, he would be devoted to her. His life would be spent making her happy. How could he do otherwise if she saved everything he held dear.

But Spin's raised brow said she smelled something fishy. Before he could decide how to convince Spin that his intentions were good, a crash sounded overhead followed by a spine-tingling roar and then a heartrending cry of pain.

Zhi took off. He forgot about Parker and Spin. He had to get to his mother before that beast could do her any more harm.

He raced up the stairs, climbing to the third floor where they'd secluded him so that he could hurt no one but himself. But he always got to her. Mainly because his mother wouldn't leave her husband alone.

Lin sat outside the door, trembling as she

hesitated. She had been with the family all her life. She knew better than to go in and get between them.

Zhi's mom was on the ground, holding a shaking hand to her face. A trickle of blood spilled through the space between her index and third finger. His father held his food tray up high, preparing to launch it at her. Zhi went for the tray.

He subdued his father. The old man balled his fists and threw some punches Zhi's way. They were ineffective.

Still, Zhi wanted to punch the monster. He'd cost this family so much hurt, anger, pain. This was all his fault. All of it. He'd ruined so many lives with his selfish ways. And he wouldn't have to pay for any of it now that it was coming due. The old beast deserved to hurt for his crimes.

All it would take would be one blow from Zhi. That would be enough to end it all. The former duke's features sobered when he looked up into his son's eyes. Like the coward he was, he cowered before his fully grown and capable son.

Zhi saw the fear in his father's eyes. But worse, he saw his reflection in his father's gaze. The sight reminded Zhi of looking up at his father while the enraged man towered over him as a boy.

No. That wasn't Zhi. That would never be him.

Slowly, he caught his breath, but his glaring eyes never left the old man. "Mark my words, for I'll only say this once, touch her again, and I will send you to an institution. The cheapest one with the worst reputation that I can find."

The fear in the old man's gaze told Zhi he had heard him. That despite his memory and sense stealing disease, that Zhi would not have to repeat himself again.

With that settled, Zhi turned to tend to his mother. He searched until he found where she lay on the floor. But she wasn't alone. She was in Spin's arms.

CHAPTER SIXTEEN

$\mathcal{A}$fter racing up to the third floor behind the duke, Spin froze at the threshold of the open door. From the corner of her eye, she saw the maid, Lin, trembling and shaking her head. Her once perfectly coiffed bun now dropped at her shoulder, slowly unfurling as the wisps of hair escaped capture. Instead of heeding the maid's warning, Spin stepped over the threshold of the room.

Inside, she found a gruesome scene. There was a monster lying on the bed. Zhi towered over him, a look of pure hatred in his eyes.

It should've scared her. It didn't. What had scared her was the prior expression that had darkened his features. She'd raced behind Zhi after seeing the light going out of his eyes and a look of terror spread across his face.

She knew that look. She'd seen it before. She'd felt

its cold heart lick at her heels when she was a kid. So, she'd race up the stairs behind him and onto the forbidden third floor. Into a scene, she'd seen too many times before.

It was an unfamiliar face, but the expression of the monster in the bed was all too familiar. Contempt, fear, and insecurity were all scratched up in the haggard lines of his features. His eyes, so like Zhi's, landed on her, and Spin flinched under his scrutiny. Then Zhi was there, blocking him from her view.

With the trance broken, Spin returned back to the present and the aftermath. Something had been thrown. There were shards of glass on the floor.

Her mind worked to put the pieces back together. The porcelain handle gave away the mystery. A teacup had been thrown.

The fragments revealed another mystery. There were drops of blood on the fibers of the lush carpeting. Spin followed the sanguine trail to the trembling woman.

Spin had to shake herself again. To bring herself back to the present moment. To remind herself that it was not her mother this time.

Crouching down like approaching a wounded animal, Spin made slow movements toward the woman. But there was no need for caution. She could tell the woman wasn't the type to ever lash out. She was the type to take what was thrown at her as her due. In fact, one of her delicate hands reached to pick up the cup's handle. She halted when her own blood touched her fingertips.

With gentle fingers, Spin took the cup from trembling hands and set it aside. The woman turned to face her. Spin saw Zhi looking back at her.

This was the woman from the portrait. The one with the brightest look of love in her eyes. That light had gone out, probably long ago.

Blood trickled down the side of the duchess' head, threatening to spill into the corner of her eyes. Spin unwrapped her head scarf. It was freshly laundered, so she didn't worry about any contamination. She was meticulous about her care for the few items she did possess. Folding the scrap of cloth, Spin pressed it to the duchess' cheek.

"No, my dear, don't." Her voice was like feathers floating down from a clear, blue sky. "Please don't ruin your things for a scratch."

It wasn't a scratch. It would likely need stitches. Spin was certain the staff and her son would have to fight the duchess to seek care outside the home. So, she would have to use underhanded tactics to press an insignificant bandana to the woman's head.

"You have such beautiful eyes," Spin said. "Just like your son's."

The shame retreated from her beautiful face at the compliment that referenced her son. But not entirely. The duchess' smile was tentative. But it provided a momentary distraction. The hand she'd raised in protest lowered, allowing Spin to press the cloth to the trickle of red on her temple.

"I saw the painting of you and your family in the hall," said Spin. "I stopped in my tracks when I saw how beautiful your smile was."

"You're very kind to say so." The duchess winced, and then closed her eyes and gave over to Spin's care.

Spin knew the drill. If she addressed the issue of the moment, the woman would retreat inside herself. Just like her mother would've done.

With the blood cleared from her wound, Spin saw that it wasn't as bad as it looked. It wouldn't need stitches after all. Just some antiseptic and a Band-Aid.

The duchess' eyes were still closed as she allowed Spin to mend her wound. A solitary tear formed at the corner of her eye. Before it could drop, she swept her tear away. Spin had the overwhelming urge to open her arms and hug the woman to her.

"Thank you, my dear," said the duchess. Her voice was so soft, like broken china. She took the bloodied bandana out of her hand. "I'll have this laundered for you."

"*Mǔqīn?*"

The duchess lifted her head to her son. "I'm okay, darling. It was just an accident. I slipped as I was serving tea. I'm such a clumsy woman."

Zhi's jaw tensed. His eyes glazed over. It was as though his eyelids closed. But they hadn't. He was staring with them wide open. Spin had her own pair of shuttered lenses that turned the dark world a fake rosy gold.

He came over and offered his mom a hand. As she rose, Spin had to stop herself from reaching out to help the older woman up. Somehow, she looked even smaller as she rose.

Zhi made to steer her out the door, but his mother circumvented his efforts. She went instead to the bed. Her husband recoiled as she leaned over him. He hadn't needed to.

Spin looked away as the duchess leaned over to plant a kiss on the man's forehead. His eyes closed as she did. They remained closed as she rose.

When the duchess joined Spin and Zhi at the door, she was all regal smiles. "You both get cleaned up while I see to dinner."

Zhi kept his strong jaw closed. His gaze still glazed.

"Yes, ma'am," said Spin. "I'm sorry, I mean yes, Your Grace."

She tried another curtsy. A real one this time. But she'd never been any good at it, and so it looked as though she were squatting before a personal trainer, and doing a bad job of it.

"Sorry," she said after the poor display. "I was raised in America."

"You did just fine," said the duchess. "And you may call me Nian, my dear. I'll see you at dinner."

Spin and Zhi stood silently as they watched Nian walk away. Spin turned to Zhi, but he was still in his rose-gold state of denial. When she was younger, she resented being pulled from that place before she was ready, so she turned on her heel to leave him be.

"I'll go find Lark," she said.

Before she took a step, his hand halted her. His fingers were gentle on her bare skin, but their heat seared her. She was certain he'd leave a mark.

"Thank you," he said quietly.

Spin kept her eyes on his fingers. She wondered if that's where his calluses came from? From protecting his mother from that monster.

"Don't mention it," she said.

He didn't let her go. She chanced a glance up. His gaze connected with hers.

In his clouded gaze, she saw clear understanding. He might struggle with communicating with the cultural slang of the club, but this language between them he understood perfectly. They shared a common language of dysfunctional homes.

After one more lingering look, Zhi bowed his head. Then he straightened and turned.

"Hey," she called after him.

He stopped and glanced over his shoulder at her.

"No texting or DMing without me." She wagged her finger.

A small smile quirked at the corner of his lip. He gave her a quick nod. And then he was gone.

A second later her phone chirped. The peace-sign emoji popped up on her phone.

CHAPTER SEVENTEEN

*D*inner was entirely civil and a bit surreal. Zhi sat back and watched his mother make idle chit chat with Spin and Lark as though the earlier scene had never happened. He had changed his clothes. His mother wore a pale plaster on her temple. Spin sat with her hair free of the bandana, and they spoke about such mundane things as the weather, the sweetness of the meat Lin had prepared, and the refreshing citrus in the lemonade.

Lark made up the bulk of the conversation. He'd caught the magician's assistant glance at his mother's temple exactly once, but she never brought it up. Zhi doubted Spin had told her friend about the incident. In fact, he knew she hadn't.

He wasn't sure how he was certain. But he was. Likely, it was the same certainty he'd had when he'd stood next to her after ... the incident.

No one had ever stood by him and his mother's side during or after one of his father's rages. The staff knew better than to get between them. Nian would always defend her husband. She'd once threatened to sack a footman who had come to her defense. Soon everyone simply waited until the dust settled to clean up the mess the nobles had made.

Not this time. This time, Spin had been by his side. She'd tended to his mother as though she'd done it all before. He got the feeling that she had. But for herself? Or for someone else?

He was dying to ask. But he wouldn't. Just as they'd made a silent agreement to not speak of what happened earlier today, he knew he couldn't ask her about her past.

In the present, his mother was peppering Spin with questions about her life and getting nothing. Spin wasn't shutting the duchess out, not at all. In answer to one of the duchess' questions, Spin would say something vague and turn the conversation toward Lark. Lark always had an interesting tale to tell. When the conversation came back around to Spin, she'd smile and redirect the question to his mother.

Zhi sat quietly, watching the DJ work the room. She was masterful at distraction. She mixed and spun the record away from her every time the needle of a question was dropped. By the time the dishes were cleared, he realized he knew not one more fact about the woman than he had before he'd sat down.

Again, he wondered what she was hiding? Why wouldn't she share any of herself? The woman he'd seen back in the music room, she had been the real Spin. He was sure of it. As she'd layered the different beats one on top of the next, he'd been granted a peek inside her world.

There he saw a woman who was complex. She could be soft and airy like the notes she pressed on the piano. But she could be loud and raucously annoying like the repetitive percussive beats of the polka. She was also loyal and inclusive like the way she'd had Zhi clap along to be part of the song.

She was all these things rolled into one. But pull them apart, and you didn't get the whole picture. Zhi wanted to know more. He wanted to turn the volume of her up and learn the words to her score.

"Begging your pardon, Your Grace?"

Zhi looked up to see Oswald at the dining room's entrance. He still wore his service coat. Zhi couldn't help but see it was threadbare. The staff didn't usually have to worry over that so much as guests were an irregularity here at the estate. But Oswald and the rest of the staff had had to don their tired uniforms for the entire day so as not to tip off Spin that there was anything amiss. He couldn't have her tell Parker the true state of his affairs.

"There is a matter that needs your attention," Oswald demurred.

Zhi held in his sigh. He knew that any matter that

needed his attention would require him to get his hands dirty. He rose, bowing to his mother and inclining his head to the women.

Before he stepped away, he caught Spin's eye. Her penetrating gaze made him think that she knew what was up. But she couldn't. She might be a translator for him between two worlds. But she didn't know his inner thoughts.

He felt the doubts touch the corners of his eyes at that thought. She'd seen so much of him and his private world. If he wasn't careful, she would see it all. He turned from her, shutting off her view of himself, and proceeded Oswald out of the room.

"What is it now?" he asked once they were out of earshot.

"Best if I just show you."

Zhi had been neglecting many of the repairs while Spin and Lark were in residence. He didn't want them to catch him in his overalls getting his hands dirty. He'd tried to keep them from the third floor, but that hadn't worked.

Spin had found out the big secret of his parents, something he hadn't discussed with even his closest friends. Though he knew that Alex and Carlisle had always known there was trouble at home. There had been similar trouble in their own homes. Zhi supposed that's what happened when people didn't marry for love.

He and his friends rarely spoke of their troubled homes. They went wild outside of it instead. Now, Alex was settling down, happily in love and engrossed in a new business. Carlisle wasn't looking for love. The baron-to-be's every waking moment was spent on saving his own family's business and fortune.

Zhi wondered if he could tell Spin the truth about his intentions with Parker. It was clear the two weren't an immediate match. But Zhi was determined to make the woman happy if she'd give him a chance.

He still needed Spin's help with ensuring that chance. Perhaps she could help him make a mixtape. Was that still a thing? The thought of sifting through music with Spin warmed him. It soothed the tension that had been building in him since leaving his father's room.

"Here we are," said Oswald.

Zhi snapped back to attention and closed his eyes with a groan.

Oswald had brought him down into the basement. The exposed pipes before him were corroded and leaking. He could hear the strain on the metal. Zhi pinched the bridge of his nose, the tension returning.

"It won't hold much longer," said Oswald. "We'll have to get a professional in if there's any hope of keeping our heads above water."

"Let me give it a try first." Zhi stripped off his jacket and got to work. He might be able to get the pipes under control for a few days, a few weeks at most, but if he didn't solve the problem soon, everything would burst.

CHAPTER EIGHTEEN

Spin watched from the corner of her eye as Zhi rose and strode from the room. When his gaze had caught hers, she'd felt her heart quicken. Her mouth had gone dry, and suddenly her lower lip felt the need to be tugged into her mouth for moistening. Something passed between them, she didn't know what, but it was something.

She didn't like it.

He'd been quiet through dinner. She'd felt his eyes on her the whole time. Each time she'd deflected a question about herself and redirected the conversation to Lark or back to Nian, Zhi's eyes had never left her face.

Spin got the feeling that he knew she was hiding. Worse, she was certain his lowered lashes told her that he wouldn't let her hide from him. She'd avoided his gaze until that last moment when he'd bowed to her, and their gazes had caught and held.

Tearing her gaze away had been a chore, but she'd done it. Now she'd need to tear herself away from him. He had no idea that he'd gotten closer to her in one day than anyone had in years.

She found herself wanting to tell him that he wasn't alone in how he'd been raised by termites. Why termites? Most animals in the wild weren't monogamous. Termites were some of the few.

They were known to mate for up to twenty years. Unfortunately, the lifetime partnerships had human statistics when it came to divorce. Nearly half broke up before death could part them, and when they broke up, it was violent. There were scientists who'd seen them chew the other's antennae off.

Spin wanted to tell Zhi that she understood the dysfunction between his parents. She wanted to tell him that she understood how a mother could love someone who hurt her emotionally and physically and still go back for more. She wanted to tell him that it was okay to hate his father, that he should go through with his threat to send the monster away because it would never get better.

But she had done none of those things for her own mother. So instead, she'd bit her tongue, and she'd looked away.

He left the room without knowing any of that. He'd

looked so tired, so alone. Guilt filled her heart, and she wanted to run after him.

"I hope you'll stay with us your entire stay here in Cordoba," said Nian.

Spin turned back to the duchess. Her gaze immediately went to the bandage on her forehead where antennae might have been were she of a different species.

"We're only here until tomorrow, and then we have to go back," said Lark. "I have shows and Spin … well, she always finds work."

Spin smiled evasively. She did always find work. She had the healthiest relationship with money that she knew. The secret was to not chase after it. She'd known from a young age that things came to those who didn't chase after the object of their affection.

"What is it you do, my dear?" asked Nian.

"I'm a DJ."

"Do you mean you're on the radio?"

"No, ma'am. I play records, but not on the radio. I play in clubs."

"Is this your own music?"

"It's the music of other people. I mix their songs together to make something new."

Nian's bright eyes lit up reminding Spin of the painting in the hall. "You mean like a maestro?"

"Yes." Now Spin's smile brightened. "I suppose so."

"That's simply fascinating. I studied the piano. I

was quite good in my youth. And then I met my husband, and that life was over for me." The duchess' smile was wistful and sad.

Lark caught it. She looked to Spin. Spin gave a slight shake of her head. She knew that Lark had seen the Band-Aid on the duchess' forehead.

Lark hadn't come from an abusive home, but she hadn't grown up in the best of neighborhoods. She knew the signs of abuse. And though she was the type of woman to want to call out the abuser; the one who would be in the driver's seat if a girlfriend wanted to do a drive-by on her cheating boyfriend. Lark also knew when to hold her tongue.

"My mother always said you shouldn't let a man hide your light," Lark said.

Well, she *almost* always held her tongue.

Nian's gaze began to cloud over. Before she could retreat into herself, Spin intervened. She grabbed at the first happy thought she could muster.

"I heard Zhi playing," said Spin.

And just like that, the duchess' face lit up again.

"We had a little jam session earlier," Spin continued.

"You played with him?" Nian frowned as though she were confused.

Spin nodded.

"He's never played with anyone but me."

Spin told the butterflies in her belly to take a hike.

That didn't mean anything. She'd barged in on him and sat down without an invitation. He was too polite to kick her out. Never mind that he'd clearly enjoyed their session.

"I do hope you stay longer," said Nian. "This house was once filled with guests. But now ... that my husband is ill ...we don't get very many."

Spin noted the chips on the plates. These weren't the finest. She'd been in a big house before. These were the types of plates used by servants. The forks were actual silverware and not gold plated. There was a ducal emblem on them, but like something that might be sold in a gift shop. The meat served had not been the choicest cut. The butler's uniform was frayed.

Nian rose. Lin materialized from the doorway. The maid's bun was once again a tight circle of neatness. But her black uniform was more slate gray than black, as though it had been washed more than its fair share of times.

"I'm going to check on my husband and retire for the night."

Spin and Lark rose as the duchess made her way out of the room.

"She's really nice," said Lark once they were alone. "Are you going to tell me what's going on with that bruise on her head?"

"Not my story to tell."

Lark nodded in acceptance. "Too bad we can't stay

longer. This place is like a fairytale, but we have to get back to the real world. Did you book the tickets yet?"

"I'll get to it." Spin still wasn't quite ready to tell Lark she wasn't heading back with her. No reason to ruin the day. Not since it was practically over. She'd just wait until tomorrow.

CHAPTER NINETEEN

Once again, Zhi started the day drenched in water. Although this time, it was mostly sweat. After a long night and early morning, he'd won another round with the pipes. Only just barely.

He'd graduated from YouTube with the DIY problems he was facing. A real plumber would have to be called in soon. Or they'd all have to grow fins to stay in the house. Or maybe it would be easier to clean the pool and use that as a water source.

He didn't care so long as he got himself dry. But as he headed for the grand staircase, he heard feminine voices rounding the corner. He slunk back beneath an alcove just before Lark and Spin came into the front door with shopping bags.

"You didn't have to buy this for me," said Lark.

"It's cute on you," said Spin.

"You're too generous with your money."

"You know my philosophy on money. It's better spent than kept."

"That's only because money seems to find you no matter how much you give it away."

Zhi waited for the two women to pass. While he did, he kept his eyes on Spin. Something passed over her face at the talk of money. It was a curious conversation. Just like everything about her.

She clearly didn't come from money. She lived a bohemian lifestyle. She seemed to detest excess. But she was happy to spend it on her friends. The woman was a walking contradiction.

When the coast was clear, Zhi slunk to his room. Turning on the shower, he hesitated as the pipes groaned. But the water came through. He stepped beneath its spray, thankful for the heat. He soaped up and washed the grime of the last day off. He wanted to luxuriate for an hour or so, but five minutes was all he gave himself. He didn't dare try his luck with his patchwork pipe job.

Toweling off, he went to his wardrobe. He itched to slink into something comfortable and entirely informal. Unfortunately, as long as guests were on the grounds, he had to play the part. So he pulled on slacks that hung a little loose on him. The toes of the shoes he stepped into pinched. There was a thread loose on the tail of his shirt, which he tucked in.

Once presentable, he stepped out of his room and headed down to properly receive his guests. The girls were nowhere to be found. He found himself a little disappointed at the empty hall.

He pulled out his phone and tapped the Instagram app. He could send Spin a DM, but he decided against it. What had she said about waiting? He was too impatient to remember.

He had no clue why he was feeling so agitated. He was hanging out with Parker tonight. He should be focused on that.

Looking up, he found himself outside of the music room. The door was cracked open. His heartbeat picked up when he heard the first notes from the keys. But his pulse quickly settled as he recognized the tune and its player.

Zhi came into the room, closing the door behind him. His mother didn't mind being heard. She just didn't prefer to be watched as she played.

When she saw him, she changed her tune. Sliding down to one side of the bench, she began a partner song. Zhi sat on the other end of the grand instrument and picked up his part. The music wasn't so loud that they couldn't converse.

"I like your friend," said his mother.

"Spin?"

"What an interesting name."

"Says the woman who named her son a letter of the alphabet."

"I suppose her name is Elle." His mother's lithe fingers moved quickly over the keys for her part.

"Why would you think that?" Zhi's fingers moved slowly as they accompanied her in this part of the melody.

"Spin d'Elle."

He paused, losing his place in the music to consider that.

"The two of you get on well." His mother hedged. "She's a musician, you know."

"I do know." Zhi picked the melody back up. The song picked up speed as they held their conversation.

"It's nice to have things in common with someone."

"What are you on about, *mǔqīn*?"

"I am glad one of your friends is willing to help our family out with our ... difficulties. It frees you to follow your heart."

Zhi tripped on the keys, missing a beat. His mother's playing didn't falter. She changed the song, playing a solo tune now that his fingers were frozen.

"The king is marrying a girl for love," she said. "The prince too. Both women aren't noble. That widens the field for you to find someone you truly care about."

Instead of setting his mother straight, Zhi swallowed past the lump in his throat. She had the right of it. Just the wrong woman.

"You know that I love your father ..."

Zhi gritted his teeth and focused on regaining feeling in his hands. He flexed and closed his fingers, trying to pump life back into them.

"Your father's sense of duty was bigger than his heart. That was always fine. I had enough love for both of us. But I'd like my son to experience love over duty."

Zhi didn't answer. He felt his mother's eyes on him. He knew if he looked at her, she would see the truth. He wasn't going to have a love match. Like father, like son, his duty would trump his heart. The difference would be that he would make his wife feel loved, unlike his father had done with his wife.

With the feeling back in his fingers, he joined his mother once more at the keys. They made it so joining the opposite ends of the keys made a new harmony. Much like he'd done with Spin the other day.

As they came to the finish, his mother's part in the song trailed off until he played the resounding last note. The silence lasted for only a second before applause sounded from the door. Zhi looked up to find Spin holding her phone in one hand while clapping her wrist with the other.

"I hope you don't mind, I recorded that."

Zhi's breath caught in his throat. Recorded it? How much of it?

But one glance at Spin settled his fears. Her eyes shone bright like they had when they'd played together. She'd only heard the music.

"It was beautiful," she said coming into the room, her gaze focused on the duchess. "May I have your permission to use it in a song?"

Nian's eyes lit up. "How flattering. Of course, my

dear. Do you know, I have a recording of one of my performances."

"I didn't know that you performed," said Spin.

"It wasn't in public. It was in a recording studio. I fear I was too shy to play while others watched."

Nian pulled a record from the shelf of music. She moved to the ancient record player in the corner. Spin went to the device with awe. The needle dropped, and a hauntingly beautiful sound began.

Spin's eyes lit with recognition. "It's Bach."

Both Zhi and Nian looked at her in surprise.

"*Concerto Number Five?*"

Nian nodded, clearly impressed. Zhi had to admit he was too. This woman kept surprising him and throwing his assumptions about her back on their heels.

Spin closed her eyes. "It's beautiful."

Zhi couldn't take his eyes off her. Her joy of the music would forever be ingrained in his mind. He was having trouble reconciling this woman who liked to play harsh, electronic notes with the woman enthralled by his mother's playing.

"Zhi Wen, dance with her."

Spin's eyes slammed open. "Oh, no. I'm not one for waltzing."

"It's simple. Show her, darling boy."

Ever the dutiful son, Zhi stepped up to Spin. He held out his arms. At first, he didn't think she'd take his offer. But after a moment, Spin put away her phone and held up her hand. He clasped her fingers into his grasp. Electricity zinged into the center of his palm and spread like a storm through his blood.

With his other hand, he placed his fingertips on her waist and felt the same sparks. Spin gasped as he pulled her close. And then they began to move.

It had been so long since Zhi had danced like this. It had been forever since he'd felt like this. All his cares were swept away as he moved her around the floor. He forgot about the pipes. He forgot about his finances. He just took a moment and joyed in moving in synch with the woman in his arms.

CHAPTER TWENTY

Spin had never been swept off her feet. She'd never wanted to be. Couldn't understand why any woman would. She couldn't run if her feet weren't on the ground.

As a little girl, she had steered clear of the fairy stories and myths. Reality was too vivid and loud in her world. But twirling around in the arms of the Duke of Mondego, she let the scars of her childhood fall away.

For just one moment, she imagined what it would have been like had her life been different. What if her prince had come? What if a knight had swooped in to rescue her and her mom out of the dragon's claws?

She might've danced as a young girl instead of escaping into music. She might've dined on fancy dishes every night with different things to eat instead of Oodles of Noodles. She might have met a man like Zhi and been content to stay in his arms forever.

But that wasn't her life. Not then and not now. So when the beautiful song his mother had captured with her fingers ended, Spin let Zhi's hand go.

However, it wasn't that easy. Their fingers had become entwined at some point in the dance. So though she yanked, she had to wait for him to loosen his grip on her. Before he could loosen his grip, he had to release her from his intense gaze. Before he could release her from his gaze, she had to stop staring at his mouth.

"Oh, that was lovely," said the duchess. "You move so beautifully, my dear, like you were born on a ballroom dance floor."

"I wasn't."

Spin jerked her gaze away. She yanked her fingers from his grasp, causing them both to wince. She took a large step back putting distance between their bodies.

"I was born in my mom's bed because we were too poor to afford a doctor."

Spin stared at the floor in the silence. She never told any details about her life. She rarely brought up her mother. In less than twenty-four hours, these two people knew more about her than anyone else alive.

She supposed it was fair. She knew their secrets. Which meant neither would say anything about the other. Mutually assured destruction it was called.

"And anyway," Spin lifted her gaze, a grin replacing

the lost look in her eyes, "that's not how we dance in the clubs. We shuffle."

"Shuffle?" asked the duchess. "Like the 70's dance?"

"Something like that."

Spin pulled out her phone. Her thumb flicked through her playlist. A hard, electronic beat sounded from the device's speakers.

Nian winced and frowned at the song. Zhi lifted a brow, his frown mirroring his mother's expression. Spin began the simple steps of the club dance. The shuffle was comprised of moves that even the rhythmically challenged could accomplish. She made a motion for Zhi to follow her. After a moment he fell in line.

The duchess sat back watching them. A slow smile spread across her face. Spin had seen that look before. It was the look of a meddling mama who liked the match she saw.

Recognizing that she'd stepped into a trap, Spin tripped. Zhi caught her. She'd tried to get away from the possibility of a pairing, but there she was in his arms again.

The music cut when her phone beeped an alert. Spin stepped away from Zhi to tend to her phone. It was a message from Instagram. She tapped it to see Parker's face come up.

"Is everything all right dear?" asked the duchess.

"A friend of mine and Zhi's has invited me out to

dinner before the club." Spin held up her phone so that Zhi would see Parker's profile.

That snapped them both out of the moment they'd shuffled into. Zhi reached into his back pocket for his phone.

Spin watched as his thumb swiped and swiped. His frown increased. Clearly, he didn't get an invite.

It was becoming clearer and clearer that Parker wasn't that interested in the duke. But seeing as Spin couldn't have the duke take too much of an interest in her, she began to tap on the keys of her own phone.

Hanging with Z right now. Having a great time.

Parker typed back: *Bring him.*

Spin's thumb slid down from the top of her phone which announced its half battery life and typed: *Can you send him the invite. Phone about to die.*

A moment later, she heard a chirp from Zhi's phone. She cast a glance up at him. He wasn't grinning as though he'd won the dating lottery. But he did look relieved.

Good. She'd get the two of them together in one room. She doubted it would lead anywhere, but it's what she promised. And then she'd be taking off. Starting a new life. In someplace new.

"I see you two are headed out to do young people things," said Nian.

"Yes, we are, mother. Don't wait up."

Zhi went over and kissed his mother's head. She brought him down for a hug.

Then she looked at Spin. Nian opened her arms. Spin hesitated. But she'd been raised to mind adults.

Spin walked over to the older woman on unsteady feet. She bent down to be enveloped in the duchess' small arms. But the hug went all through her, reminding Spin of her own mother.

Nian held her tight, and then tighter for another second that Spin hadn't realized she needed.

"I'm so happy you came to stay, my dear."

Spin was too choked up to say anything. So, she just nodded. Then made a quick exit. She went back to her room.

Lark was outside somewhere with Mathis showing him a few magic tricks. Spin pulled out her suitcase. She hadn't unpacked. She never did. Everything was set for her to go. And she would be doing that later tonight. Best to just slip out without saying goodbye to anyone.

CHAPTER TWENTY-ONE

After three wardrobe changes, the two women and Zhi made it out of the house. The women had been ready in only fifteen minutes. It was Zhi who'd had to perform the outfit changes.

Spin had vetoed the suit and tie he'd initially put on. He'd argued that it was a designer brand. She'd cocked an eyebrow and told him that unless it was Supreme or Bape, he wasn't leaving the house with it on.

Zhi didn't know who either of the designers were. But he'd dutifully gone and changed. Next, he'd come out in jeans and a starched t-shirt. He hadn't missed the feminine smile of approval on Spin's face. Even though she'd wiped it off to shake her head in the negative to tell him that he was trying too hard to look cool.

His next venture out was a happy medium. He'd put back on the slacks and kept the t-shirt. He did a turn for Spin, feeling oddly warm at the thought of her eyes on him. He'd been on display before. He was a catch in the upper echelon circles of Cordoba, though no one knew of his financial straits.

Spin wasn't after him for the money he didn't have. She wasn't after him at all. She was simply helping him because ...

"Why are you helping me?"

Her gaze traveled up the length of him. Under her perusal, Zhi felt the ridiculous need to flex. He could tell she appreciated what she saw. He didn't quite understand his pull to this woman.

She had a rough exterior. But he'd seen past it to the soft refinement of the insides of her. Her arms around his mother and the soft way she spoke to her rang in his ears. The feel of her in his arms as they waltzed. Then the feel of the music they'd made rushing through his veins filled him.

Spin shrugged, not quite meeting his gaze. "It's my good deed for the day."

"You've helped me for more than a day."

"So, my cup runneth over. And ... you'll do."

Before she could turn to walk away, Zhi put out a hand to stop her. He felt a tingle in his palm where he'd capped her shoulder. Spin tensed in his hold. He wanted to knead her shoulder and remove the tension.

He wanted to pull her back in his arms and waltz with her again but with his front to her back this time. He wanted to sit beside her, shoulder to shoulder, thigh touching thigh, at the piano and make more music.

"Thank you," was all he said.

Spin looked back over her shoulder at his fingers resting so close to her collar bone. Her lips parted and closed. Her tongue snuck out and moistened her lower lip, but still, she said nothing. Still, he didn't let her go.

"Thank you for all of it," he said. "For helping me, for helping my mother. But especially for making polka palatable."

She breathed a laugh through her nose. Her lips quirked up in a smirk. And then they flattened.

"You're a good guy," she said finally. "Parker's going to be a lucky woman."

She stepped away from him then. Zhi's palm itched at the empty feeling. He flexed his fingers, but he didn't reach for her again.

They didn't speak again as they joined Lark. They climbed into Zhi's sports car. Spin dove into the back, leaving Lark in the passenger seat.

Lark chatted amiably with Zhi. She was a great conversationalist. Zhi saw why Spin kept her around. The woman easily filled the silences that Spin seemed to prefer.

Zhi was happy to let Lark talk while he pondered the contradiction of DJ Spin d'Elle.

Elle. It was a pretty name. He wondered if it was hers. It didn't suit her.

He knew so little about the woman. But again, she didn't know the whole truth about him. Still, he felt like she knew him best in the world at the moment.

In the rearview mirror, their silent communication continued. Spin rolled her eyes at one particular story of Lark's. Zhi raised his brow at another story that was particularly incriminating about the two women. Spin narrowed her gaze as though to say she'd neither confirm or deny the tale.

"When are you two headed back?" he said. "Not that I'm kicking you out. You're welcome to stay as long as you like."

"I need to get back by Wednesday," Lark answered. "I have a show Thursday."

"So, you'll stay another night?" Zhi asked.

"We can't impose on you," said Spin.

"It's no imposition at all. We all love having you, especially my mother. She doesn't get out much with ... my father being ill."

Zhi's gaze darted to Lark. There was a question on her brow, but she didn't ask it. So, Spin had kept his secret, even from her closest friend. He felt humbled that he'd gained her loyalty in such a short time.

"We're here," said Spin, her gaze out the window.

Even though it wasn't technically open yet, there was a line snaked around the corner of Omar's club. Zhi turned his car over to the valet. Before he could reach for the back door, Spin had already alighted from the car. He narrowed his eyes at her, but she shrugged and moved past him. Zhi went around and handed Lark out.

"Don't mind her," said Lark. "She thinks chivalry is an 80's band."

Zhi chuckled and offered his arm for Lark. She took it gratefully. They came up to Spin in the line.

"You're welcome to wait in the line," he said to her. "Or you can take my arm and go inside."

Spin huffed out a breath and crossed her arms. Zhi shrugged and turned on his heel with Lark. As they approached the front of the line, he felt Spin's hand on his arm. Again, his body went alive at her touch.

"This is total elitism," she muttered.

They entered the club. Strobe lights nearly blinded Zhi. The base pulsed through him. But it didn't cause an immediate headache. He was able to pick out the various parts of the beat this time, all because of his time making music with the woman at his right arm.

Looking down at Spin, he saw that light in her eyes. The one where she was clearly enjoying the music. Already getting lost in it. He wanted to go there with her, but someone came into his view.

"You guys made it."

Zhi tore his gaze away from Spin to find Parker coming toward them. Parker pulled everyone in for a hug, starting with Spin. When she opened her arms for Zhi, he went to her. Parker was thin in his arms, and warm, but there was no fire of electricity. At least not at the moment.

"Isn't this amazing?" Parker said when she pulled away.

"Yeah, it's pretty lit." Zhi snuck a sideways glance at Spin.

She gave him one of her half smiles of approval.

"It's PLUR all over the place here," he went on.

An elbow to his ribs shut his mouth. The look on Spin's face clearly told him that he was now overdoing it. So, he shut his pie hole.

"You're looking pretty fly there, your dukeness." Parker ran a hand down his shirt sleeve.

"Thank you," he said. "You're looking pretty dope yourself."

"Come join us. We're over here."

Lark walked beside Parker toward her table. Zhi set to follow them until he noticed Spin wasn't beside him. He turned back to her. "You coming?"

She shook her head. "I'm gonna hit the dance floor."

Zhi stepped up to her so that she could hear him over the music. "What if I need you?"

Something sparked in her eyes at his comment. He felt his own cheeks heat at his needy admission. He hadn't meant it that way. Had he.

"You won't," she said after a long moment.

He didn't like how final that sounded. He wanted

to protest. He wanted her at his side, like a security blanket on his first day of school.

"She's digging you now," said Spin. "Don't pretend anymore. Just be you. If she doesn't see how cool you are, then it's her loss."

If only it were that simple. Zhi desperately wanted to explain his predicament to Spin then. He wanted her to understand the dire straits he was in. But she turned from him and got lost in the crowd. Zhi felt lost standing without her.

Duty tugged at him. He turned and headed to Parker's table. Once there, Parker scooted over and made space for him. Zhi took the seat.

Parker smiled at him.

Zhi smiled back at her.

He opened his mouth to speak, but nothing came out.

Parker turned her attention to the person on her left.

Zhi turned his attention back to the dance floor.

He caught a flash of Spin. Her eyes were closed as she moved in time to the music. Beside him, he heard Parker ask him a question. But he couldn't tear his gaze away from the woman on the dance floor.

Spin was completely unguarded as she moved. All her defenses were down now that she was lost in the music. It was as though he saw the burdens lifting off her shoulder as the beat dropped.

He envied her that. He was always able to get lost

in the music from the piano when he or his mother played. The melodies were the only things strong enough to lift his cares away. He had the urge to join Spin out there, leave it all on the dance floor. Unfortunately, another man stepped up behind Spin to take the place Zhi hadn't claimed.

CHAPTER TWENTY-TWO

The beat vibrated from the speakers into the air. The base urged Spin's feet to move. The treble lifted her hands over her head. She shimmied her shoulders and swirled her hips to the melody, shouting the repetitive lyrics of the popular song at the top of her lungs.

It was exactly what she needed. To get lost in the music. To find solace in the beats.

The problem was that the only thing the pulsing rhythm did was to heighten her senses. Her fingertips still burned where she'd placed them in the crook of Zhi's elbow. Her cheeks were still hot from the blast of his breath as he'd spoken to her. Even though she closed her eyes, she still saw his eyes gazing down upon her with need before she'd pulled away from him, and he'd turned to Parker.

Spin wrenched her eyes open, staring straight into

the neon lights. She hoped it would laser off the memory of him from her vision. It didn't.

Like a beacon, she found Zhi across the room. He sat behind a table roped off with velvet. Waiters served small plates of food meant for sharing. Parker leaned her elbows on the table as she talked to the person on the other side of her. Zhi's arm was behind Parker on her seat. But his head was turned from Parker. His eyes were on Spin.

Spin felt their connection even across the room. She saw the shift in his pupils as he watched her move. She saw the flare of his nostrils as his gaze traveled to her lips.

This connection between them was insane. It had to be broken. He wanted to be with another woman, a woman whose body was turned from his.

If it wasn't clear through their brief interaction on the ship, or in their sparse direct messages in which Spin was often the intermediary, Parker had zero interest in Zhi. Zhi had nothing in common with Parker. Spin couldn't fathom why he wanted her so badly?

From her place on the dance floor, Spin stared into his eyes trying to see if she could suss out his reasoning. Zhi had everything. On the outside.

Inside his house was a different story. His father was abusive. His mother was compliant. His home needed repairs. On top of all of that, why would he want to bring a woman who didn't understand him into the mix?

From his place at the dining table, Zhi's gaze narrowed. His lips turned down in a frown as he held her gaze. Had he heard her thoughts? Were they speaking telekinetically now?

No. That wasn't it at all. Zhi's frown came not from their connection to each other.

Spin smelled him before she felt him. A sweaty clubber had stepped up behind her and was matching her moves. The problem was that she didn't want a partner.

Not on the dance floor. Not later outside the club at a rundown ducal estate. She was a loner. She was used to being on her own. It was better that way.

Spin turned around to tell the guy slipping into her personal space to take a hike. She met with empty air where the sweaty clubber should've been. Instead, he was on the ground. Zhi towered over him, a menacing look on his aristocratic features.

"Keep your hands to yourself," Zhi shouted over the music. He hadn't needed to shout. The warning radiated from his face.

"I was just dancing." The man started to get up. Then thought better of it and stayed down.

The music didn't die down, but the dancing did. All eyes in the club were on the scene of the threesome. It was more attention that Spin hadn't wanted.

She turned and marched away from the prying eyes. Passing the DJ booth and speakers, she headed toward the back of the club. Once the heat of the stares was off her back, and the music volume was a distant thud, she took a deep breath. But she wasn't alone.

"Are you okay? Did he hurt you?"

Zhi's hands were on her shoulders. His fingertips grazed the exposed skin there, and she shuddered. Spin whirled to face him, taking a step back and out of his embrace as she did so.

"What is wrong with you?" she shouted.

Aristocratic brows dipped down in annoyance at her. "He had his hands on you."

"We were dancing."

"You didn't look like you wanted him there. Or did I read that wrong?"

No, he'd read it right. He'd read her right. That wasn't the issue. "I don't need rescuing."

His brows softened, but the frown of confusion stayed in place. "I never said you did."

"I do fine on my own. I don't need some duke in shining armor coming into my world to protect me. I can fight my own battles."

It was a low blow. One he could interpret as being aimed at his mother. It could have been. But Spin's true aim had been at her own mother. Whether Zhi knew her intention or not, his voice softened when he reached out to her.

"I think you're the strongest woman I know."

It was his thumb brushing across her cheek that broke her. A single tear slid down her cheek. Zhi caught it with his thumb. He tilted her chin up so that she was staring into his eyes, eyes that saw everything. She was no longer hiding, and neither was he.

His descent was slow. At the last second, he veered from her lips, and his lips brushed her cheek, tracing the trail of the tear. Slowly, he moved over until his lips met hers. He gave her ample time and space to get away.

She should've run. It was what she was good at. But her feet refused.

For the first time in her life, Spin stopped running and held still. She felt something she'd never felt before, contentment. She'd be content to stand in this spot for the rest of her life waiting for this man to kiss her.

She'd have to wait a longer time. A millimeter before his lips met hers, a breath before she knew the wonder of his taste, Zhi pulled away.

He let out a long sigh. But he didn't let her go. He pulled her into the cradle of his arms. He bent down to rest his face in the crook of her neck, breathing her in.

"I should not have done that," he said. "That was weak of me."

Spin felt weak herself. She didn't have the strength to hold her walls up any longer. They were all crumbling down for this man. She had never understood how her mother had left herself so vulnerable for one man, until this moment.

She was going to kiss the Duke of Mondego. If he asked her to stay in Cordoba longer, she was going to say yes. If he asked her out on a date, she was going to go. She might even wear a dress.

"I used to think my mother was weak." Zhi made the admission at the cone of Spin's ear. "For taking every insult, every ..." He drew in a shaky breath. "Every blow from that monster. It took me a long time to see that he was the one who was weak."

It wasn't kissing time yet. It was confession time. Spin let out a slow breath, finding the patience as well as the courage to admit her own truth.

"You never know what makes them stay," she said. "Especially when you want them to leave the monster so badly."

She'd never admitted that much to anyone. She hadn't felt the need to go into details. By the way Zhi tightened his hold on her, she knew that he understood.

Unlike with the Mondegos, Spin's mother, Angelica, had been abused by a man who hadn't even claimed her. She'd stayed for years. Until finally, she found the courage to leave. Leaving Spin's father had taken a lot of strength for Angelica. Staying away had taken everything.

"My mother would do anything for me," Spin said.

"She would have endured anything to keep me provided for."

Spin didn't know why she needed to say it, but she needed him to understand. She turned her head and looked up into his pained face. With just one glance, she saw that he clearly did.

"I understand that," Zhi said. He brushed his callused fingertips across her brow with reverence. "I'd do anything for my mother, including ignoring my own heart."

"Ignoring your heart?" The prickle of cold doubt spread across the tops of her shoulders. She was loath to pull away from Zhi's warmth. She held on as she reached for clarity. "Are we talking about me? Or is this about Parker?"

Zhi took a deep breath, but it came out shaky. He turned back to where he'd come, back to where Parker was. The look on his face when he turned back to Spin was filled with pain, guilt, and shame.

Spin's first instinct was to gather him up in her arms, to take all his pain away and bring it into her. But she wasn't her mother. She'd learned that strength came from standing up for yourself and not sitting down or taking the blows from another person.

"You're going back to her, aren't you?" said Spin.

Zhi shut his eyes. When she tried to step back from him, his hold tightened. But only for a second before he loosened his grip, and she was able to easily break away.

It was déjà vu. How had she come to live her mother's life? Every time her father went back to his wife, her mother had stayed in bed for a week. A few weeks later, he was back. Finding them wherever they were in the world and the cycle began anew.

"I have to," Zhi said, bringing Spin back to her present reality.

Spin's feet were already in motion. There was no way she would willingly enter a cycle of her own. But she turned back. She had to know. "Why?"

Zhi looked sick, shame-faced.

"You have everything, can have any woman," Spin said when the answers didn't come soon enough. "Parker doesn't want you. Why are you after her? Is it because you're both rich?"

He actively avoided her gaze now. Turning his head away so that she couldn't see into his eyes. But she didn't need to see him to know.

Spin stepped to him, forcing him to look at her. Her gaze caught on his hands and the callouses there. There was a new cut she hadn't noticed before. How did a man of leisure get cuts and calluses?

There was a single thread loose on his collar. Her father had always dressed impeccably. She'd never seen him in the same shirt or pants twice. That was the way of the noble class. So why was Zhi constantly bucking those traditions?

The possibility that flashed into her head made

her nauseous. "You're not rich, are you? You're after her money."

He reached for her then. "It's not like that."

She raised a brow.

"The situation is," he clarified. "But I'm not like that."

Spin crossed her arms over her shoulders. Even as he began to confess, and she began to see him anew, she still ached to be inside his arms.

"I'm not going to be like that. I'm not going to be like my father. I'm going to make her happy. I'm trying to learn how."

As his lips worked on detailing the devotion he'd have for another woman, Spin still wanted to feel them against her lips. She wanted to know what he tasted like, what he felt like.

"I can't let my mother live in squalor. I can't let the staff lose everything. I'm not doing this for me. I need to save them."

It was rational. All so rational. The sickness she thought she would never catch, the illness she'd always believed she was immune from, raged like a high fever through her body.

"I'll do everything in my power to make Parker happy."

"That's the worst kind of abuse. You're abusing yourself." Spin took a deep breath. Her stomach hurt, and her chest was hollow, as though she'd just risen from the worst flu of her life. "You're not the man I thought you were."

She lifted her head to regard him. The proud head of the Duke of Mondego hung in disgrace. He looked as sick as she felt. But he didn't take a single word of it back. He looked resolved to his fate.

To his credit, he didn't ask her to accept his decision. Good. Because she couldn't. She never would.

She did what their mothers hadn't had the strength to do. She turned on her heel and walked past him. Not once did she falter or look back.

CHAPTER TWENTY-THREE

*H*e was only able to lift his head high enough to watch her walk away. He felt like he was coming out of his body. His feet wanted to run after her. His hands balled into fists. His heart beat as though it were trying to chase after her. His head told him to stay rooted.

He didn't know what to do. He didn't know where to turn. He felt pulled in every direction.

In the end, duty won out. He couldn't abandon his family and his home. He had a responsibility. That was paramount. It was what he was born to do.

The moment Spin was out of his sight, his chin slumped to his chest from the weight of his actions and what he still had to do. With feet as heavy as cement blocks, he turned back toward the club. When he reached for the curtain that separated the club floor from the back, it was yanked open to reveal Omar.

"What are you doing back here?" said the marquis. "The party is that way."

"Yeah. I'm headed back."

"You don't look like you're having a good time."

Zhi could only take a deep breath. He couldn't think up a response.

Omar put a hand to his shoulder. It was a light touch, but Zhi felt he was about to fall over from the pressure he felt.

"Looks like women troubles," said Omar. "You chasing after that pretty DJ?"

Zhi's glance shot up. He opened his mouth. To deny it? To bemoan it? He wasn't sure. His features screwed into incredulity. How had Omar known?

"It's pretty clear you two have a thing going. It was clear back on the ship. You even had the whole completing each other's sentences thing going on like you walked out of a romantic comedy." Omar shuddered. The entertainment producer did not like that particular genre of media. Not enough testosterone to hold him in his seat, he'd once explained. "You two have a falling out? She realize you're just a man and put your pants on one leg at a time?"

"I wasn't chasing after Spin," Zhi admitted. "I was chasing after Parker."

"Why would you bother with her?" Omar frowned. "You two have nothing in common."

"Why does everyone keep saying that."

"Maybe because it's true."

"And me and Spin have so much in common? She's a DJ. She doesn't have a permanent address or a bank account. I don't even know her real name."

Omar shrugged off each of those concerns. "I don't know if you have a lot in common, but you two certainly have chemistry. But hey, it's your life. Do with it as you see fit."

That was just it, it wasn't his life. It was other people's lives that he was managing. It was other people's messes that he was cleaning up. If he got the chance to live his own life, it wouldn't be in this lifetime.

He was too tired to explain any of that to Omar. The man had amassed his own wealth outside of his family's fortune. His parents were happily married. He wouldn't understand, and so Zhi stormed past his old friend.

Once back out near the speakers, Zhi had to face the music. The base made his head throb as he walked toward Parker's table. She didn't look up when he approached. Her attention was on the woman beside her. Or maybe it was a guy. The other person's hair was closely cropped, but they were wearing makeup. This world of Parker's was truly confusing.

"Parker?" He had to call her name twice, louder each time to be heard over the music before she looked up.

"Hey," she said when she turned to face him. "You wiling out out there?"

Zhi wasn't sure what that meant? Was she asking him if he was ready to go? And if so, did she mean on his own? Or with her?

As the beat changed, Parker threw her hands. "OMG, this is my jam. Let's dance."

Before he could wonder if she was talking to him or the person next to her, she grabbed Zhi's hand and tugged him out on the dance floor. She began the shuffle step dance. He knew this. He could do this.

With sure steps, he fell in line next to her. Her steps were a little different than Spin's. Parker added hand movements and hip swivels that Spin hadn't shown him. He kept with the basics. But after a few repetitive verses, it got old quick.

He looked around at the moving, glowing, rainbow bodies. What was he doing here? Was he consigning himself to a life of this?

He leaned close to Parker's ear. "Can I talk to you?"

"What?" she shouted as she moved about the dance floor.

"Can we talk?"

He was standing motionless in the center of the dance floor and getting dirty looks. Then he was jostled to his left when someone shuffled by. Finally, Zhi put his hand at Parker's low back and guided her off the floor.

"What's up?" she asked when they were away from the booming speakers.

"I just wanted a minute to talk to you."

"Okay." Parker looked up at him expectantly, giving him her full attention for the first time since they'd met.

Now that he had her alone, he didn't know how to begin. Except with the truth. "You have no interest in me, do you?"

"Interest?" she asked. "What do you mean?"

Nope. She didn't. He knew enough to know that if he had to clarify it, she didn't feel it. "I can't do this."

Parker put a hand on his arm. There wasn't a single spark where her bare fingertips touched his skin. "Zhi, what are we talking about? Where's Spin? Did you guys have a fight or something?"

His ear prickled at the sound of Spin's name. His heart didn't skip a beat, it thudded at the front of his chest. "You think there's something between me and her?"

Parker cocked her head as she regarded him. "It's pretty obvious."

Was it? Why were his feelings for Spin obvious and not his pursuit of Parker?

"You two always had your heads together on the ship," Parker continued. "Then you invited her to stay with you. If you're not an item, then I don't know what?"

But he and Spin couldn't be an item. He had

responsibilities, a duty. A duty that would make him as unhappy and miserable as his father.

Looking down at Parker, Zhi saw the truth. He'd make this woman unhappy and miserable. He'd never hit her or say an unkind word, but being with someone when he had feelings for another was a kind of abuse.

Spin's voice sounded in his head. *That's the worst kind of abuse. You're abusing yourself.*

"I'm sorry," he said.

"What for?" asked Parker

"For what I almost did to you."

"To me?"

"You haven't seemed to notice, but I've been trying to seduce you."

Parker burst out laughing. Then sobered. "Oh. You're serious. Zhi, you know I don't play for your team?"

He had no idea what that meant? Another reason this relationship would never work. He needed an urban dictionary just to understand this woman.

Parker put her hands on his shoulders and turned him around. "Go find Spin. She's the one that needs the seducing."

But Zhi hesitated. He could go and find her. And then what? He had nothing to offer her. And he'd have the baggage of his family and staff coming along with him.

CHAPTER TWENTY-FOUR

Spin walked slowly down the dark streets.

The day had just turned over to dawn. She'd walked all night, her pace slowing more and more. But no matter how slow she walked, Zhi hadn't caught up to her. She had to face facts; he wasn't coming after her.

Her lips still burned from the almost kiss. It wasn't as though she hadn't been kissed before. But she'd known it would've been perfect, and she couldn't stop thinking about the perfection of what would've been. She knew his lips would've fit over hers perfectly like they were the key to her lock. She'd hungered for his breath to mix with hers. She'd known just the taste would've given her life.

It was the other reason she was walking so slowly. She had every urge to run back to him. To run back to a man that had said out loud that he planned to use a woman for her money.

Zhi had admitted that he was after Parker, not for her heart, not because he had real feelings for her, he was after her wealth. Spin had been so wrong about him. It didn't matter what his reasons were. He was contemplating it.

Though it had seemed to pain him. Though he'd looked tortured as he'd gripped onto Spin all throughout his confession. Though he'd only been able to bring himself to let her go when he'd reminded himself of who he was doing this for; his mother and his staff.

It didn't matter that his reasons were honorable. If he went through with it, he'd be no better than his own father. And it looked like he was going to go through with it. He had likely turned back to his pursuit of Parker since he hadn't come after Spin. Nor had he slid into her DM.

Her phone hadn't buzzed in all the time since she'd walked away from him. Even Lark hadn't checked after her. Though Lark was used to Spin disappearing at all hours and for long stretches.

This would be the longest stretch in their acquaintance. Lark might miss Spin when she was gone, but it would take her a while to realize Spin was gone for good. Then it would likely not take very long for her friend to get over her absence.

That was the way Spin had always moved since her

mother's passing five years ago. She didn't get attached to anyone. People could only disappoint someone if they opened their heart.

It was the one good lesson her father had taught her. People could only hurt you if you let them. Spin had never let anyone close enough to hurt her.

Her time here was up. She'd stayed too long, both here in Cordoba with the duke and in Nice with Lark. Spin would slip into Mondego House and grab her perpetually packed bags. Then she'd slip out into the rising dawn and be gone like a ghost.

As she approached the towering estate, a town car pulled up. Spin recognized the vehicle. It was the same one they'd pulled up to the estate in. It as the marquis'.

The luxury car rolled past Spin. Stopped. And then reversed. The door opened, and Lark bounded out.

"You'll never believe what happened to me last night," said Lark.

She was breathless, her eyes sparkling. She brought Spin into her arms and squeezed her tightly. So much for Spin's quiet and goodbye-less departure.

Spin tried to remain motionless and not receive the affection, but after walking alone for hours, she needed it. She brought her arms around her friend and relaxed into the embrace.

Lark made to pull back, but Spin was still holding on. When Spin tried to collect herself and let go, Lark squeezed her tighter.

"What is it?" said Lark. "What's happened?"

"It's nothing." But Spin's voice trembled.

"It's definitely something." Lark pulled back but didn't let her go. She peered into Spin's eyes. "What did he do?"

"He?"

"Zhi? Did you two have a falling out?"

Spin looked at Lark in confusion. She opened her mouth to deny that there was anything between her and Zhi, but she knew it was pointless. How had Lark known?

"It was obvious that you two had a thing for each other," Lark answered the unspoken question. "I figured he went off with you after he left Parker at the club."

"He left Parker?"

"Yeah," said Lark. "You do realize that Parker isn't into men?"

Spin was still reeling from the fact that Zhi had left Parker at the club. Maybe he'd come to find her? Maybe he was in the house waiting for her?

She turned to the massive front and hurried up the steps. Entering the house, both Spin and Lark were met with chaos. There were buckets everywhere catching water as it fell from the ceiling.

The staff looked up at the door with expectant gazes that fell when they saw Spin and Lark standing there.

"Is he with you?" said Oswald.

"Who?" said Spin.

"The duke?" Oswald was visibly upset.

"We've reached a critical mass," said Mathis. "I don't think his skills can repair this."

"We can't call a plumber," said Lin. "We can't foot the bill."

"If we don't do something, we'll all be underwater," said Lin.

Spin looked up at the water falling from the sky as things began to fall into place. She thought back to Zhi's calloused hands. She thought back to his words from last night. It looked like things were more dire than he'd let on.

"I have money," said Spin.

All eyes turned to her. The only sound in the hall was the *plip-plop* of water into quickly filling buckets.

"From my pay from my last job working for Parker."

Spin heard a groan behind her. But it wasn't Lark this time. It was the pipes. They sounded as though there were ready to burst.

Oswald's gaze was wide with worry, but his voice was firm. "We can't let you do that. The duke would never agree to it."

The duke had considered seducing a rich woman to fix his problems. Spin wondered if the staff knew of his plan. She doubted it. Just as they seemed certain he wouldn't take her money, she got the impression that they thought too much of their employer to repeat the mistakes of his father.

"I'm not using the money," she said. "You need it more than I do. Call the plumber."

Oswald hesitated. Luckily, his wife didn't. Lin was on the phone, dialing the number before Oswald even opened his mouth. She handed the phone to Oswald as it began ringing. Oswald grabbed the receiver and began to speak with the person who answered.

As the staff gathered around the phone and corralled the buckets, the doorbell rang. With everyone else up to their elbows, Spin turned to get the door.

As she walked to the great door, she wondered where Zhi was. Where had he been if he hadn't come home last night? Was he out searching for her? But all thoughts fled her mind as she pulled the door open and came face to face with the crepe-thin man from the hostel.

He opened his mouth. Then paused as he squinted at her. Before she could think to run or shut the door, recognition dawned in his beady gaze.

"This is fortuitous; two birds in one net," he said.

Spin swallowed, but the lump in her throat was too big. Her heartbeat raced, and her stomach felt like rocks were dropping into her gut boulder by boulder.

"Lady Eleanor Trent? I've been looking for you."

CHAPTER TWENTY-FIVE

Zhi stared down into the waters off the pier. The small waves of blue lapped at the wooden structure as he stood watching the first ship of the new day sail out to sea. He'd been there when the last one had lifted its anchor. She hadn't been on that one either.

He'd called the house when he'd left the club, but no she hadn't come back. Neither Spin nor Lark was there. He'd walked the streets last night searching for her. She had been nowhere to be found.

He'd slid into her DMs, but she hadn't responded. He didn't have her actual phone number to call her, to talk to her. He needed to talk to her. He needed to tell her.

To tell her what exactly?

That he was in love with her? Was he in love with her? He wasn't sure? Was this pounding of his heart, this breathlessness, this yearning need in his fingertips, this thirst in his mouth, was all this love?

He didn't know? All he knew was that it would not abate until he found her. Until he had her in his arms again.

He'd sensed the first time they'd met that Spin was a runner. There were only two ways off the nation island of Cordoba. The next flight to France wasn't for a few hours. But there were boats headed out before that. As a last resort, he'd come to the docks. He'd looked into the face of every passenger that boarded the craft.

No one had had her fire. No one had had that crooked smile. No one had had that silent communication that the two of them shared. Instead of finding a kindred spirit in a single glance, they'd all glared at Zhi as he invaded their privacy.

He'd waited until the last person had boarded the first boat of the day, still looking each person directly in the eyes, still not finding the connection he sought. He stayed for long moments after the ship had sailed.

Had his own ship sailed? Had he lost her for good?

He reached for his phone again, readying to slide into her DM. He'd Gram her. He'd Snapchat her. Heck, he'd rebuild Myspace if that's what it took to find her and beg her forgiveness.

He'd beg her for another moment. Beg her to mix music with him. Beg her to simply look in his eyes and know exactly what he was feeling.

He'd gotten it all wrong earlier when he'd tried to use words to explain his situation. This time he'd simply hold still and open his world to her, to show her what was truly in his heart. She'd understand then. She had to.

Then they would have a whole new reality to contend with. He had no clue how he'd save his family and home now. What he did know was that there was no point in saving it if he'd lose himself.

Looking down at his phone Zhi saw that the device was dead. Made sense as he'd been tapping on it all night long. Unfortunately, there were no charging outlets on the pier.

He decided to head home. Perhaps she'd gone back to Mondego House in the early morning hours. She'd have to collect her things.

Pulling up at the front of the estate, he saw a white van with a colorful cartoon plunger painted on the side. There was a plumber parked outside the house? Things must have gone from bad to worse while he was gone. He had no idea how he'd pay for this.

No, he did know. He'd put the place up for sale. He'd turn the keys over to Mr. Schiessl. After the sale of the estate and the paying off of debts, there might be enough money left over for a modest home. Perhaps a townhouse with enough space to house his mother and two rooms for the small staff who depended on them. His father would have to go into state care. There was no other way around it. But first, he had to find and fix things with Spin. Whatever was between them, he knew he wanted a future with her.

Walking into the house, Zhi came face to face with Lark.

"Where have you been?" she demanded.

Zhi ignored her quip. If she was there, then Spin had to be too. The two women were best friends. Spin wouldn't leave Cordoba without her.

Relief surged through him. He wasn't too late. He could spare a moment to deal with the disaster raining down on all their heads.

"How bad is it?" Zhi asked Oswald who had walked up behind Lark.

"It's bad," said Oswald. "But not as bad as we thought. They said they can repair it in two days."

"Where are they?" asked Zhi. "I'll speak with them about the bill."

"The bill is taken care of." That came from Lark. He'd nearly forgotten the woman was there. She had that way about her where she could blend into the scenery like a chameleon. "Spin paid for it with the money she got from DJing Parker's cruise."

Zhi closed his eyes. On the one hand, he was thankful that she cared enough to help his family. On the other, his shame reached his hairline that the damsel he'd distressed was now acting like his hero. He needed to find her immediately.

"Where is she?" he said.

"She's not here," said Oswald. "She left with Mr. Schiessl."

The man's words made no sense. "Schiessl? He took her?"

"He said he had business with her. He called her Lady Trent."

CHAPTER TWENTY-SIX

"It doesn't matter what you say to me, I'm not going back."

Spin plopped down in the plush office. Her arms were crossed over her chest. There was mud on her boots that she'd tracked through Schiessl's office and she was happy for that. She loved putting a tarnish on fine things. But only things that belonged to snobby people.

She'd been a blemish her whole life, having been born the illegitimate child of an Austrian aristocrat. Though the noble class had been abolished in the last century, her father's family still held tight to their fortune and their stuffy values.

The Earl of Feldkirch, Jakob Trent, had had no children with his wife. He had no love with her or anything in common with her except their blue blood. Or so her father had told her mother. And that wasn't until Angelica had found his wedding ring in the back pocket of his pants.

Angelica had been her father's piano tutor when he was in his twenties. Spin had learned that her father took up many hobbies and left them after his head was turned. Her mother was one of those hobbies. Unfortunately, he kept coming back around for his forgotten toy only to discard her again and again.

Her mother had endured it. Angelica endured anything for a crumb of her father's attention. Her father rarely spared Spin a glance.

It had gone on that way her entire life. Until her mother had died just before Spin had turned eighteen. To her shock, her father had sent for her. Instead of heeding his summons, Spin had run.

And now he'd found her. She had no desire to be caught in his web, to be pulled out and then discarded when he grew bored. She didn't need anything from him, wouldn't accept any of the crumbs he'd lay at her feet.

Mr. Schiessl eyed her with cool disregard. "Your father is dead."

Spin blinked. Had she heard him right? Dead?

She sat back in her chair, pressing her hand to her chest. She felt her mother's necklace laying across her heart. It was the first gift Trent had given to Angelica and the last thing that Angelica had given to Spin. The only reason Spin had kept the sordid gift was because of how close it had lain to her mother's heart.

Spin waited to feel some sort of emotion. Anything. All she got was numbness.

"He passed away nearly a year ago. I've been searching for you since that time."

A year? Last year was the first time she'd held still for longer than a few months. After all that, she'd been found on accident. Wrong place and the right time.

"He's dead?" Spin said the words. She didn't know if she needed confirmation or consolation. She just knew she had to say the words to make them real.

"I'm ... sorry?" Mr. Schiessl looked entirely uncomfortable with the condolences. "I was given to believe you two didn't have any relationship. With you being ..."

"A dirty little secret," she finished for him.

Mr. Schiessl inhaled. "Be that as it may, Eleanor—"

"My name is Spin."

"Lord Trent provided for you in his will."

"He what?" Now Spin sat forward. Her fingers grabbing the sides of the chair in a death grip.

Spin knew that her father had offered her mother money to get rid of her before she was born. She knew that he'd offered to put her away in a boarding school, out of his sight so that he could have all of Angelica's attention. It was the only thing her mother had fought him on. Angelica wouldn't be parted with her daughter.

For all her faults, Spin's mother wanted no part of the man's money, only his affection. She'd strove to prove that to him time and time again. Though Spin didn't think her father ever believed her.

Whatever money he gave, her mother gave most to charity, after she took care of whatever she and Spin needed for themselves. Spin hadn't grown up poor. But she grew up with a healthy distaste for money after her father had used it against her mother her entire life.

He'd come to her after her mother had died. Not to the funeral. Of course, he couldn't be seen mourning his longtime mistress. But he had come to Spin and offered her a check to disappear, to keep her mouth shut about who and what she was. He had to keep up appearances.

Spin had yanked the check from his hold, ripped up the slip of paper, and tossed the shreds in his face. Then she'd taken a bag and disappeared.

And now he was dead and still trying to buy her off. Whatever amount it was this time, she would do the same. She'd tear up the check and toss it in Mr. Schiessl's face.

"Your father has left you a sizable sum."

Schiessl produced a slip of paper. Spin snatched the check. She was in the process of tearing it to shreds when she caught a glimpse of another set of documents on Schiessl's desk. She couldn't see the particulars, but she saw the name Mondego in angry red letters.

Her thumbs released from the brittle paper. She handed the check back to Mr. Schiessl.

"I don't need this."

The man's mouth opened to protest. Before he could get any words out, Spin continued.

"Someone else does."

CHAPTER TWENTY-SEVEN

Zhi sped down the streets, thankful for the horsepower in his car, uncaring of the speed limits on the street. He wasn't one for breaking the law, but if the authorities came after him, he would definitely use his connections to get out of the jam and get to where he needed to be.

Blessedly, the streets were mostly empty at the early hour. The cops must still be at breakfast. He made it to the address on the solicitor's card faster than a magician could pull a rabbit out of his hat.

Zhi parked, taking up two spaces. He leaped out of the car, uncertain if the door had closed. He hadn't changed or showered. Not because of the plumbing, which was still being repaired. But because he didn't care. Getting to Spin or Eleanor or whoever she was, was more important than anything.

He raced into the building, shirttails hanging out,

shoes muddy from his time on the pier. A glance in the door's window showed his hair was completely out of place.

He charged past the receptionist and marched up to the door with Schiessl's name on it. Zhi's frame filled the doorway of the large office to see the tall man surrounded by a stack of papers.

"Where is she?" demanded Zhi.

Schiessl didn't even look up at him. He shuffled some papers around on his desk looking entirely put out. "I assume you mean Lady Trent."

"So, she is noble?"

The solicitor's eyes rolled, though he still didn't look up. "In another time period, no. But with today's loose morals and laws, yes. Lady Eleanor Trent, the illegitimate daughter of Lord Trent of Feldkirch of Austria."

Zhi didn't care about any of that. He only cared to find Spin and bring her into his arms. To show her the man he was now, the man he would be because of her. No, not just because of her, because of everyone he cared about.

Those close to him didn't care about his title or wealth. His friends liked him for who he was, not the numbers in his bank account. His staff stayed because they believed in and respected him. His mother loved him.

And Spin? She hadn't been interested in any of the trappings around him. She'd been dragged into liking him because of the connection between them. It was unseen like a chord struck on a keyboard or strummed on a guitar. He couldn't see it, but he felt it resonate through him.

Zhi turned back to the solicitor. "Just tell me where she went."

The man shrugged. "I don't know? She didn't say."

Zhi was back where he started. But she came back to the estate once. Perhaps she'd come again. It was entirely possible that they were ships in the night who had passed each other by again. Lark had said her bags were gone, but surely Spin wouldn't leave without talking to one of them.

There was a little juice in his phone now. He'd plugged it in while he'd driven there. Zhi tapped on the social media icon for Instagram, preparing to send her a message. He looked up to see that the solicitor held up a small rectangle that looked like a check.

"She left this for you."

Zhi stepped forward. It certainly was a check. The small piece of paper was an extremely large check.

"What is this?" Zhi said.

"Her inheritance. She left it to you."

"Me?"

"She left it to the Mondego estate, to be precise. It's enough to cover all your debts."

For a brief second his heart soared. They were saved. His family, his legacy, they were all saved. But then his stomach clenched as he did the tally. They may have been saved, but at what cost?

If she were going to leave him this check she could've put it in his hand. She could've come back to the house and put it in his mother's hand. Why would she leave it with the solicitor?

He knew the answer. It turned his stomach and stopped his heart. The answer was because she had no intention of coming back.

Zhi had gained everything and lost it all. But he wasn't giving up. He had to get her back. The estate was a house. Spin had become his world. He just had to find her and tell her so.

CHAPTER TWENTY-EIGHT

pin scrolled through the tracks on her song list. The most played over the last two weeks were sappy love songs and angry chick music. But further down the list were classical songs. Songs she fell asleep to every night.

Her finger hovered over the delete key that would put the songs in the trash bin. In the end, she lifted her thumb. It was an empty gesture. The songs were in the cloud, just like her head was.

Spin brought the beat down, bringing her set to a close. The set she'd played in the warehouse club hadn't moved her. Her feet hadn't left the ground. Her head had stayed present. She'd woven the beats seamlessly, setting the crowd on a melodic fire, but she couldn't get lost in the music she'd made.

Applause jolted her thoughts. She stepped off the raised platform as a nondescript track played while the main event set up. She'd been playing in these small underground clubs across Cordoba for the last week, making just enough cash to afford a place to rest her head each night.

It was all she needed. Just a bed. Food had no taste. She couldn't hold a conversation with anyone. She could barely hold another's glance for longer than a few seconds.

Everything about her felt heavy. Especially her heart. She was a walking cliché. But she'd get over it.

Clearly, Zhi had. He hadn't contacted her on any social media. He'd taken the money and run.

She knew she should do the same, run that was. But she couldn't bring herself to board a plane or boat, even though now she had enough money for a ticket.

Spin pinched the bridge of her nose. When she opened her eyes, she saw a dark figure standing in front of her. She yelped and jumped back.

"Hey," said Lark. Her voice was nonchalant. Her hands on her hips as she regarded Spin.

"I told you to stop doing that."

The two women glared at each other. Then Spin's heart lurched. She was here. Spin wanted to pull her friend into her arms, but Lark's hands were crossed over her chest.

"No, you stop," said Lark. "You're the one that pulled the disappearing act this time."

"How did you find me?"

Lark rolled her eyes. "Like it was hard. You're not as

good as you think. Especially in your profession where you play loud music. Of course, we heard you."

We?

"The real question is why did you think you had to run? What did you think I'd do? You know my parents aren't perfect."

Lark knew. Of course, she knew. She'd been standing in the hall when Mr. Schiessl had announced her real name.

"I've only ever belonged to my mom," said Spin.

"Well, you belong to me too," said Lark. "We're bonded for life. No matter where you might end up, we're family."

Spin's heart felt hot. The corners of her eyes pricked with tears. They reached out at the same time and folded themselves around each other. Lark hugged Spin so tightly that her feet left the floor. Spin breathed Lark in, and her head filled with sparkles.

"What are you still doing here?" Spin said when Lark pulled away. "You have shows back in Nice."

"I got a new gig."

"What new gig?"

"I'll tell you later. Right now the next guy's up."

Spin didn't care about the headliner. She only cared about her friend and what their next step would be. Because it would be together. Spin didn't want to be alone anymore. Neither did she want to leave Cordoba. She wasn't ready to be off this island and away from all of its people just yet.

She was ready to tug Lark out of the club. Then she heard the first notes from the speaker. Spin's head turned slowly, carried by the lull of the notes. Lark had said *we*.

The first notes of the piano made her feel like she was floating on air. Her gaze lifted, and she saw him. He stood over a keyboard, his lithe fingers moving swiftly but lightly.

He said he never performed in public. But there he was in a suit and coat with a graphic T that said *You Spin Me Round.*

Zhi looked into the crowd, finding her gaze. He smiled down at her with that crooked grin, and her heart burst open. He winked, turning his attention back to the instrument before him. He lifted his hand and flicked a switch and then the unmistakable notes of a polka sounded.

The crowd, which had taken a few tentative steps towards the dance floor, came to a dead halt. When the electric beat mixed in between the sound of the keys and the strings of the polka, a few heads bobbed. Then after a few minutes of the harmonious beats, the bodies began to move in earnest.

Spin swayed but not to the beat. Her steps were to get herself closer to him. When she got to the stage, he reached for her and brought her into his arms. Had the world been spinning before this, because everything was calm now.

The polka died out to be replaced by a popular

track. Zhi swept Spin into his arms and to the back of the stage. He was there with her. Parker was nowhere in sight. She had his full attention. But hadn't she always?

"I would've done that a few nights ago," he said. "But the organizers made me audition and then wait for an opening. In the end, I had to put in a call to Omar."

"You absolutely passed my test."

His grin spread. He pulled her closer. More than anything Spin wanted his lips on hers. But there were things to be said.

"I need you to know that I came after you," he said.

"I can see that," said Spin. "It was some grand gesture, playing in public like that."

Zhi shook his head. "No, before. That night. I went back and sat with Parker at first. But I couldn't …"

He shook his head again, not completing that sentence. There was no need. She understood what he meant.

"It was only a second before I came after you. By the time I got home, you were already gone."

Spin swallowed. "There was something I had to take care of."

Zhi brushed a tendril of hair from her temple, and she closed her eyes at the slight touch. "I'm sorry about your father."

Zhi cradled the side of her face in his palm. With

his other hand, he brought them closer together. The gem at her neck between their hearts.

"But, my darling, you can't use your father's penance to pay for my father's mistakes."

"That's not what I was doing. I was trying to save your family."

"You're my family now. Or, at least, I'd like you to be."

Her lips parted. The desire she had for this man growing more urgent with each passing second. Once more, she knew what it was to belong to someone. Not because of blood, not because of money, because of their hearts.

Still, she couldn't let him throw his legacy away. Zhi was one of the good ones. He was a truly noble man, someone who should be a peer of the land.

"But your home," Spin protested.

"It's just brick and glass. I'm selling the estate."

"Zhi, no."

"Let me finish. It's being turned into a music school. My mother will teach piano. There will be classes on every instrument and every category of music, including polka and DJing."

Spin laughed. She lifted her hands to rest on the side of his face, mirroring his own motions. They stood like that gazing down at each other for long seconds.

"What about your dad?" asked Spin.

"My mother has agreed to put him in hospice

nearby. She visits him every day, but she's no longer his full time caretaker. I can see some of the life coming back into her eyes. Maybe one day, she'll remember that her life is her own, and she'll start living for herself again."

It was what her own mother had attempted. But Angelica had only tasted such freedom for a short time before she'd passed away.

"We need to write a new chapter," he said. "Score a new song. You and me."

"I'd like that."

"Good, because there's space for you. In my home. And in my heart."

"I've been looking to put down roots somewhere. I'll start with your heart."

"It's all yours."

He tilted her chin up and slanted his mouth over hers. They kept their hands on each other's faces, holding one another in place as they deepened the kiss and the connection that had existed between them from the first day. There were no words necessary between them. There never would be again. They understood one another perfectly. They were perfectly in tune.

ABOUT THE AUTHOR

Shanae Johnson was raised by Saturday Morning cartoons and After School Specials. She still doesn't understand why there isn't a life lesson that ties the issues of the day together just before bedtime. While she's still waiting for the meaning of it all, she writes stories to try and figure it all out. Her books are wholesome and sweet, but her heroes are hot and heroines are full of sass!

And by the way, the E elongates the A. So it's pronounced Shan-aaaaaaaa. Perfect for a hero to call out across the moors, or up to a balcony, or to blare outside her window on a boombox. If you hear him calling her name, please send him her way!

You can sign up for Shanae's Reader Group at http://bit.ly/ShanaeJohnsonReaders

The Rebel Royals series

The King and the Kindergarten Teacher

The Prince and the Pie Maker

The Duke and the DJ

The Marquis and the Magician's Assistant

The Princess and the Principal